THE NEVADA GUN

by Gordon D. Shirreffs

One by one they had eliminated the occupants of the Lazy E Ranch until it held only one lone female. It was almost theirs . . . then Vic Standish rode in to give her a hand . . . and his gun.

Gordon D. Shirreffs

THE NEVADA GUN

John Curley & Associates, Inc.
South Yarmouth, Ma.

Library of Congress Cataloging-in-Publication Data

Shirreffs, Gordon D.
  The Nevada gun / Gordon D. Shirreffs.
    p.   cm.
  ISBN 1–55504–848–X (lg. print).—ISBN 1–55504–849–8 (pbk. : lg.
print)
  1. Large type books. I. Title.
[PS3569.H562N48   1989]
813'.54—dc19   88–7990
                                                                        CIP

Published in Large Print by arrangement with Donald
MacCampbell, Inc. in the United States and Canada, the
U.K. and British Commonwealth and the rest of the world
market.

Distributed in Great Britain, Ireland and the
Commonwealth by CHIVERS BOOK SALES LIMITED,
Bath BA1 3HB, England.

Printed in Great Britain

Chapter One

The rain came down suddenly, hissing into
the hot bed of ashes and blackened metal that
was all that remained of the big ranch house
of the Lazy E. Vic Standish mechanically
loosed his slicker from the cantle straps of his
saddle and shrugged into the waterproof,
never taking his eyes from the mingled
smoke and steam arising from the thick layer
of ashes and embers. There was no sign of
life about the other buildings situated on the
large knoll overlooking the rain dappled
creek that wound its sinuous way through
Craneo Valley and disappeared in the narrow
gorge to the south.

Vic turned in his saddle and looked back
up the isolated valley that was nestled deep
in the Nevada mountains. The place was as
deserted as a lunar landscape. A finger of
mist drifted across the creek and hung about
the heavy log bridge that spanned the
rushing waters. Not a sign of life. Not a steer,
or a horse, not a man or a dog, not even a
bird in the wet sky. He looked again at the
big blackened area that marked the site of the

1

huge log house in which he had been a welcome guest so many times in the past. When he had last been there, over a year ago, the place had been alive with the shouting and laughter of the Earnshaw clan. Now the place was as empty of sound and of life as though the Earnshaws had never existed.

Vic dismounted and ground-reined his dun. He withdrew his Winchester from its saddle scabbard. There seemed nothing there to endanger him, yet he wanted to feel the reassuring weight of the rifle in his hands. He walked slowly about the area. Building after building was empty of men and of animals. The great barn echoed hollowly with his footsteps. The corral was empty but he noted that the back rails had been pulled down and many tracks of horses led into the woods that were behind the buildings. He walked partway into the dripping woods but saw nothing other than the tracks.

Vic rolled and lighted a cigarette. He stood at the edge of the woods eyeing the empty valley, thickening with writhing mist now that the rain had stopped. Beyond the swift running creek was meadowland and across the valley was the rugged escarpment that hemmed in the valley to the east. Towering over the silent valley was the peculiar rock formation that had given the valley its name when the Mexicans had probed far north into Nevada in their never ending search for mineral wealth. The rock formation was shaped like a huge skull, with lipless, grinning mouth eroded into the rock, and deep-set hollow eyes, while the top of the skull was naked of any growth. It seemed to brood over the valley. Craneo Valley. The local American ranchers and miners always referred to the isolated valley by its American translation of *craneo*. Skull Valley. . . .

"Where are they?" said Vic aloud. He walked down the easy slope towards the corral. To one side of the corral, on a high rise that overlooked the creek bottoms, was the family graveyard with the rain-blackened stones standing out sharply against the neatly trimmed grass and raked gravel pathways. Mark Earnshaw, head of the clan, had always kept it so. The Earnshaws had been in that country since before the Civil War and had fought Piutes to hold it, and anyone else who had the idea of taking it over.

Vic walked towards the house and as he did so he saw a body lying to one side of the pathway, half concealed by brush. It was the body of a big dog. Vic turned the body over with his foot. A soft-nosed slug had shattered the skull of the beast. A cold and uncanny feeling came over Vic. He looked up quickly, almost as though expecting to see someone watching him. There was no one in sight. The feeling persisted though. The loneliness of desert or mountain country had never bothered Vic Standish much. He was used to it, but there was something about the quietness and loneliness of Skull Valley that was working insidiously on his nerves.

Vic walked to his horse and mounted it, placing his Winchester across his thighs. He touched the dun with his heels and rode towards the road that paralleled the rushing creek. He had figured on staying that night at the Lazy E. It was a long and lonely ride to his destination but he had no choice. He turned in his saddle and looked back at the steaming ruins of the house. "Where are they?" he repeated. The dun whinnied softly as though he too was puzzled.

Vic rolled another cigarette. The Skull Valley War had ended three years ago when the fighting Earnshaws had held their ground, wiped out the greedy rustlers that had infested that part of Nevada, and served notice to all comers that Skull Valley was the domain of the Earnshaws. Mark Earnshaw had led a fighting corrida mostly composed of his own blood kin. His three big strapping sons, Norman, Phil and Buck, his two nephews on his wife's side, Webb and Joe

Dunlap, Mark's younger brother Bennett and his two boys, Nick and Saylor, as well as a number of waddies who looked on Mark Earnshaw like the Highland Scots looked on the leader of their clan. There had been casualties. Phil Earnshaw and his cousin Webb lay buried in the family cemetery; Bennett Earnshaw had ended his days as an invalid because of wounds received in the fighting. Saylor Earnshaw had vanished one dark night on the road home. He had not been found in two long years.

"I wonder if it was all worth it?" said Vic aloud. He had occasionally worked for the Earnshaws and several times had fought alongside them.

It was getting dark when he reached the narrow pass through which the creek cut its way to the south. The road was between the rock wall of the pass and the creek. Vic had never liked the passage of that road. It was always dark, even during daylight hours, and the wind would moan hollowly through it. In rainy weather, or when the snows thawed in the mountains, the creek would become a rushing torrent, rising high out of its banks and sometimes filling the pass many feet deep. Even now, with the recent rain of the past two days, the water was already halfway across the rutted track.

5

His vision was limited by the darkness and the winding of the pass, so he came upon the buckboard before he realized it was there. He drew in the dun sharply. The horse shied and blowed. The buckboard pole lay on the ground. There was no sign of the team. A man lay sprawled across the seat, one arm across his face. Another man lay face downward in the mud with clenched fingers dug deeply into it.

Vic dismounted and walked to the vehicle. He pulled at the arm that covered the hidden face but it was already stiffened in death. He pried it back and looked into the bearded face of Mark Earnshaw. A blackened bullet hole was in the right temple. Vic turned away, sickened by the violent death of a man whom he had always admired, and whose friendship he had valued since he had been a boy.

Bad as the sight of Mark Earnshaw had been to Vic, the recognition of the man beneath the buckboard struck him even more sickeningly. Buck Earnshaw, the youngest of the three Earnshaw boys, had the fighting heart and skill of the Earnshaws, but there had been none of the grimness of his two brothers in him when the lead was flying and the going was rough. Buck Earnshaw had had a lot of the gayer Dunlap blood in him, and he had been Vic's closest friend in the old days. His handsome face would never smile again; indeed it was hardly recognizable, for a bullet had smashed into the lower jaw and had nearly torn it off. His shirt and vest were black with blood for he had spated fully before he had died.

Vic stood up and felt the sour green bile rise in his throat. Death had been riding a pale horse in Skull Valley sometime in the past twenty-four hours. The rain pattered lightly on his slicker. He looked up and down the dim road. The pass road had always been haunted as far as Vic was concerned. Now there would be two more spirits to add to the eerie company.

There was nothing he could do, but he could not leave his two friends lying there in the rainy darkness like useless carrion. He lifted Buck into the back of the buckboard and covered both bodies with a piece of tarp he found beneath the seat. This was for the law to investigate.

Vic rode south at a faster pace as full darkness covered the cold wet country. He reached the southern mouth of the pass and looked down the long dark slopes to the south, towards Piney Creek, and his heart leaped as he saw a pinpoint of yellow light far across the wide valley. There was someone alive there at least. The dun was

7

tired but he was eager enough to reach shelter. Time and time again Vic looked back towards the dark notch of the pass. He had seen enough violence in the past year to satisfy him for a lifetime, and in coming back to the only home he knew, he had not expected to find death in full control. Violent death. . . .

The dun splashed the Piney Creek ford and Vic eyed the lamplighted window, the log house set back against the trees. A dog barked throatily and Vic grinned. "Sandy!" he yelled. The big mastiff came bounding down the road, to leap again and again high into the air, trying to reach Vic. "Take it easy, boy," said Vic. One old friend was still alive at any rate. There was still life at Jim Fancher's F Bar M.

The front door of the house opened as he led the dun through the Texas gate. "That you, Jim?" he called out.

"Vic! Vic! It's you at last! You been a long time comin', boy!"

"I'm here, Jim. I'll take care of my horse. Get me some grub will you?"

"It'll be ready, boy."

Vic stabled the tired dun, unsaddled him and rubbed him down, hanging a worn blanket on him. He fed the big horse, then carried his rifle and saddlebags to the house.

He opened the kitchen door and the warm, fragrant odour of food swarmed out to meet him. He felt a little faint, for he had expected to eat at the Lazy E.

Jim Fancher turned and grinned. He held out a big hand. "By Godfrey," he said, "this is better than Christmas seeing that ugly face of yours, boy."

Vic noted that Jim had aged considerably in a year's time. His shoulders were a little bent, his hair was almost solid grey, and his tanned face had a network of deeper lines than Vic had ever remembered. "Where's Little Mac?" asked Vic. He looked beyond Jim hoping to see Jim's partner. The little Canadian Scot who had been Jim Fancher's sidekick for many years.

Jim turned and stirred something in a pot. "Little Mac ain't here, boy."

Vic smiled a little. "Did you two finally break up after all those years of threatening to do so? Don't tell me Little Mac went home to Canada?"

Jim shook his head. He filled a plate for Vic. "Little Mac went home all right, Vic, but not quite like you're thinking."

A cold feeling came over Vic again. "He's dead?" he said quietly.

"Yes." Jim looked away. "I buried him a month ago."

"How did he die, Jim?"

"Eat first, boy."

"How did he die, Jim?"

The rancher pulled out a chair for Vic. "Set and eat," he said. "I'll fill you in."

Vic peeled off his slicker and hung it and his hat on a peg. He sat down and began to eat. "Well?" he said.

Jim leaned forward and rested his forearms on the table. "There was trouble in Skull Valley again. It's been breeding trouble again like it always has, as far back as I can remember anyway. It was like the old Skull Valley War. You were in some of the fighting in them days, boy. I guess the Earnshaws thought they had it all settled. Well, they didn't. You know how handy Mac was with blacksmithing. Well, Mark Earnshaw asked Mac to come and do some work for him and Mac rode over. Mac worked all day for Earnshaw and when it was time to come home he found his horse had strayed so Earnshaw let Mac use Earnshaw's own horse. A big bay it was." Jim's voice trailed off.

Vic stopped eating. He leaned forward. "Go on, Jim," he said quietly.

The sorrow in Jim's eyes struck Vic like the blow of a quirt. "Mac was drygulched just this side of the pass. The little man

10

didn't have an enemy in the world. Shot through the back of the head."

"By who?"

Jim shrugged. "I got ideas. I don't think they wanted Little Mac. But they saw the horse. It was dusk. They didn't take time to check to see if it was Mark Earnshaw or not and they killed the best friend a man could ever have." Jim's voice broke a little.

"They?"

Jim looked up. "I'll tell you about it later, boy. You're tired and hungry."

"*They* might have mistaken Little Mac for Mark Earnshaw and killed the wrong man that night, Jim. *They* didn't make any mistake this time."

Jim's eyes narrowed. His hand closed tightly. "What do you mean, Vic?"

"I came through Skull Valley on my way here, Jim. I found the big house burned to the ground, not a soul anywhere around, the dog lying with a slug in his head, all the horses driven off."

"No!"

"I came through the pass," continued Vic grimly, "and found a buckboard in there, with the horses gone. Mark Earnshaw was lying on the seat with a bullet hole in his head, while Buck Earnshaw lay in the mud beneath the buckboard with his lower jaw

11

almost torn off by a bullet. He died of loss of blood in a matter of minutes from what I figured. What in hell's unholy name is going on here in this country, Jim?"

Jim Fancher closed his eyes and shook his head. "My God," he said.

"Where are the rest of the Earnshaws and their kin? They won't take this thing lying down. There will be hell to pay and no pitch hot in this country, Jim."

"Norm Earnshaw traded draws in Banister two months ago, Vic. He came out on the short end. You know how fast he was, Vic."

"There was none faster in this country."

"Excepting maybe *you*, Vic."

Vic shrugged. "Quien sabe? We'll never know now. Who killed Norm, Jim?"

"A hired gun. He wasn't a Nevada man. From Arizona. Used to ride with the Hashknife outfit. Name of Forrie Cooke."

Vic's head snapped up. "Forrie Cooke? My God, Jim, he's one of the fastest guns in the south-west."

Jim nodded. "That was how they got rid of Norm Earnshaw."

"*They* again."

Jim filled coffee cups. "Funny thing. The Lazy E was pretty good rangeland, but nothing like my place here, Vic. It was the Earnshaw drive that made the Lazy E a

12

paying proposition and it took all their drive to make it so. Three months ago an offer was made for the Lazy E. A damned good offer, Vic. Little Mac and me figured if Earnshaw didn't sell, we'd maybe sell the place here, because that kind of money was too good to overlook. Earnshaw turned down the offer. Little Mac and me made noises like we'd be interested in selling. Not a nibble, Vic. Not a *single, blessed* nibble!"

"Go on." Vic rolled a cigarette and tossed the makings to the older man.

Jim rolled a quirly and lighted it. He blew a reflective cloud of smoke. "Well, there was a little hurrahing started around the Earnshaw place." Jim smiled a little reminscently. "You know how that kind of business lights the fire of battle in them Earnshaws. They gave lick for lick. I swear if you put them Earnshaws up against a squadron of cavalry or a whole tribe of Piutes they'd each pick the nearest dozen of them and charge. The hurrahing stopped, but the war wasn't over. Nick Earnshaw was killed in a bar-room brawl in Banister. Some say he was deliberately led into the fight, then done away with. No one could prove anything, but it sure looked like a rigged job."

"Who is behind all this killing, Jim?"

The rancher glanced hastily behind him as though someone might be listening. "Well, it was a combine you might call it, that wanted to buy the Lazy E. Man by the name of Jason Kile is the head of this combine. For my money he *is* the combine. Not that any of the others are weak sisters, boy."

Vic's eyes narrowed. "Jason Kile? Not the same Jason Kile who ran the Pioche country for awhile?"

"Can't hardly figure there'd be two men in Nevada with a name like that, boy. It's him all right."

"You think then that this Kile and his combine are behind the killings?"

"They want the Lazy E. They offered top price for the place. Who else could be behind the killings?"

"Seems like they won't have to do much more killing," said Vic quietly. "Who's left to fight 'em?"

Jim blew out a ring of smoke and studied Vic. "There's still Joe Dunlap, Vic."

"Joe was the weakest one of the clan," said Vic. "He'll probably sell out, if he is the last of the bunch."

"He doesn't own the Lazy E now, Vic."

Vic eyed the older man. "Then who does?"

14

"Maybe you've forgotten Peggy Earnshaw?"

Vic slowly took his cigarette from his lips. "Peggy?" he thought. "I thought she left this country."

"She came back, Vic."

"With her husband?"

"She never got married, Vic."

A cold feeling crept over Vic. "But, I thought..."

Jim shook his head. "I still say she was trying you, Vic. You were too foot-loose and fancy free to please her. I still think all that talk about marrying Dick Chapman was just to bring you to heel. When you left she cancelled out her plans for marriage and took a trip east. She came back when Norm was killed."

"Where is she now?"

"In Banister. She's been teaching school there."

Vic flipped his cigarette into the trash bucket. "Wait until she hears about her father and Buck," he said.

"God give her strength, boy."

Vic stood up. "I'll need a horse," he said.

Jim stared at him. The rain slashed against the walls of the house. "Now?" he said.

"Yes."

"You loco? Listen to that rain!"

15

Vic put on his slicker and hat. "Mark and Buck Earnshaw are lying under that rain, Jim," he said quietly. "Murdered in cold blood. I couldn't sit here tonight under a tight roof, sleeping in a soft bed thinking about them. I'm going in to Banister to notify the law."

Jim shrugged. He stood up. "Watch your back, boy," he said.

"What do you mean?"

"Why do you think I asked you to come back?"

Vic eyed the older man. "You said you needed help to run the place."

"It's more than that, Vic. I've been warned twice to keep my mouth shut about what I know."

"Who warned you, Jim?"

"I don't know, boy. You know how close I was with the Earnshaws. If I had been a younger man I would have fought with them this last hurrahing they went through. I said I thought the death of Nick Earnshaw had been rigged. Well I was in the bar-room the night he was killed. I saw what happened. I made the mistake of talking too much about it. That was the first warning I got. Then when they killed Little Mac I got to looking around, trying to find a clue as to who did the job. I was

16

getting warm when I received the second warning."

"How much did you find out?"

Jim smiled. "I'll fill you in when you get back."

Vic left the house and walked to the barn. He saddled a grey and mounted it, riding past the house. He waved to Jim as he passed the front porch. The rain misted down steadily as he rode for the crossing of Piney Creek.

Chapter Two

The yellow lights of Banister showed mistily through the slanting rain as Vic Standish topped a ridge and spurred his horse down into the wide shallow valley. He crossed the heavy log bridge spanning the river and rode towards the centre of the town. Wet hided horses stood hunched at the hitching racks outside the saloons. Somewhere up Mineral Street a mechanical piano ground steadily and tunelessly away. The lights from the fogged windows shone on the water-filled ruts of the wide street turning them into moving quicksilver. A mired wagon leaned drunkenly against the posts that held up a ramada in front of a general store.

Vic swung down from the grey and led it beneath an overhanging room. He tethered it and walked along the sagging walk until he saw the marshal's office. A light showed in it but when he opened the door the office was empty. There was no one in the building but a drunk sound asleep in a cell. If Ben Cullen was still marshal of Banister he was still up to his usual nocturnal habits. Ben made the night rounds in full faith, and if he tarried a little too long in some bars, or dallied a bit with some of the hurdy-gurdy girls on Mineral Street, that was his business. Ben was a good man with a gun, and a better politician, who had made a good job of keeping the good and bad elements of Banister living in comparative ease in the town.

He found the big marshal comfortably standing at the long bar in the Nevada Joy, with a cigar thrust into his wide mouth and a beer in his big right hand. He smiled as he saw Vic. "By God!" he roared. "Vic Standish! I thought the Piutes had killed, scalped and stuffed you! Have a drink, Vic!"

Vic nodded. "Rye," he said to the barkeep. The place was full of men. Three poker

18

games were going. The faro table was lined with players. The chuck-a-luck cage was rattling. More than just a few men looked up from their cards or their drinks to eye Vic Standish.

"Is the telegraph line operating, Ben?" asked Vic.

"Nope. Wind blew it down this side of the hills. The linesmen ain't going out to fix it until tomorrow. Why? You want to send a wire?"

"Not me. But you had better send one."

Ben's eyes narrowed. "Why? Some trouble Vic?"

"Not for me. I came through Skull Valley late this afternoon on my way to see Jim Fancher. Found the Lazy E ranch house burned to the ground, the horses gone, the dog shot. Not a soul around, Ben. Not a living or dead person anywhere around. I rode south through the creek pass and found Mark and Buck Earnshaw in there."

The saloon had suddenly quietened. A drunk was babbling and someone shut him up. The bartender placed a bottle and a glass in front of Vic and stood there eyeing Vic expectantly.

"Go on, Vic," said the big marshal.

"Mark had been shot through the head. Buck was lying dead under the

19

buckboard with his lower jaw almost shot off."

Ben Cullen shoved back his hat. He swallowed hard. "My God," he said in a husky voice.

Vic downed his drink and refilled his glass. He needed something to calm his inner feelings. "I had no way of getting them out of there. I covered them up and rode on to Jim's place. I thought you could notify the sheriff so he could get out here as quickly as possible to go over the ground for clues."

"Yeh," said Ben quietly. "Clues." He narrowed his eyes. "How long had they been dead?"

"Hard to say. They had stiffened. The house had burned to the ground but the bed of ashes and embers was still hot. I couldn't say if the house had been set afire before the two Earnshaws were killed, or after. There were plenty horse tracks behind the corral leading into the woods, but it was wet as the devil in the valley. Hard to tell when those tracks had been made."

"*You* could have timed them, Vic," said the bartender. "If it hadn't been raining that is."

"Yeh," said Ben. He eyed Vic."You still with the law?"

"No."

Ben nodded. "You see anything else?"

"It was dusk and it was raining. Anyone who had killed those two men was long gone. Unless he was watching me."

"I been expecting this," said a wizened little man standing next to Ben Cullen.

"So have a lot of other people," said a bearded miner.

Ben rubbed his jaw. "We can't get a message through to the sheriff tonight."

"I'll go back with you, Ben," said Vic.

"Tonight?"

"You aim to leave them lying out there?"

Ben flushed. "Well, I got my job here to do."

"Get me a team for the buckboard and I'll go back and bring them in myself," said Vic.

"I'll go with you, Standish," said a quiet voice.

Vic turned. The voice was vaguely familiar. He found himself looking at a man of about his own size, light-haired and blue-eyed, with a catlike look about him. "Forrie Cooke," said Vic quietly.

"You remember me then?"

Vic nodded. "It's been a few years," he said.

There was no expression on the gunman's face. "I said I'd go with you, Standish."

21

Every man in that room could feel the hidden tension between the two men who stood there facing each other. Every man in that room knew that Forrie Cooke had outdrawn and shot down Norm Earnshaw, no mean feat in itself. They also knew that Vic Standish had been an Earnshaw man before he had left the country after his comeuppance with Peggy Earnshaw. There was one other thing they all knew; the most interesting and speculative of all. Vic Standish was a fast gun. In the old days there had been speculation about Vic Standish and Norm Earnshaw as to who was the fastest of the two. That could never be proven now, but the man who had beaten Norm Earnshaw to the draw now faced a man who had liked Norm Earnshaw, who had counted him friend.

"All right, Cooke," said Vic. He looked about the room. "Anyone else?"

"I'll go," said a broad-shouldered, thick-chested man. His hard brown eyes flicked at Forrie. "O.K., Forrie?"

"It's O.K. with me, Chuck." Forrie looked at Vic. "Chuck Budd. Friend of mine."

Vic did not notice the looks in the eyes of some of the men who turned away back to their cards and their drinking. "We'll need

22

something to wrap them in, a lantern or two, and a team. Can you get the stuff, Cooke?"

"Sure. Where you going?"

Vic emptied his glass. "Somebody has to tell Peggy Earnshaw," he said quietly.

"Yeh," said Forrie.

"She lives at Mrs. Chapman's boarding house," said Ben Cullen. "That's Dick Chapman's aunt, Vic."

There was no expression on Vic's face.

"Over on Third Street," said Ben.

"Thanks," said Vic. "I know where it is." He walked out of the Nevada Joy and got his horse. He mounted it. Cooke and Bud were standing under the dripping ramada in front of the saloon. "I'll meet you here in twenty minutes," he said.

"Keno," said Forrie Cooke.

The two of them watched him ride north along the muddy street. "What the hell brought *him* back?" said Chuck.

"Damned if I know. I'll go tell Jason Kile he's back in this country. You get the stuff we need." Forrie walked off down the street. Chuck Budd rubbed his rocky looking jaw. "Vic Standish," he murmured. "Well I'll be dipped in sheep manure!"

Vic dismounted in front of the imposing boarding house that Amy Chapman had made the centre of living respectability in

23

Banister. The two and a half storey building was neatly painted, with window boxes, and neat shrubbery, white painted fences and white-washed rock garden to one side of the house. Even the trash and garbage cans placed in the driveway at one side of the house had been painted. *They* had to look respectable too.

Vic walked up on to the wide verandah and yanked at the bell pull. He saw the dim figure of a woman in the carpeted hallway through the wet stained-glass window. A moment later the door opened a crack. "Who is it?" demanded a woman's voice.

Vic couldn't help but smile a little, despite the seriousness of his mission. "Vic Standish, Mrs. Chapman."

"Oh, you . . ."

"I've come to see Peggy Earnshaw, Mrs. Chapman."

"It's getting late, young man."

"It's very important, Mrs. Chapman."

"Come back in the morning."

Vic placed a big hand on the door. "I didn't know this had been turned into a girl's seminary, ma'am. I've got to see Miss Earnshaw for a few minutes."

"You never did have any manners, Victor Standish!"

"I'm just a poor country boy, ma'am, and

never had the right upbringing for genteel manners."

"Obviously!" snorted Amy Chapman. She opened the door. "Stay right there. She can talk to you from here."

Vic took off his hat and shook the rain from it. He peeled off his slicker and stepped into the hallway. "I want to see her privately," he said in a hard voice.

She snorted a little and walked into a room at the end of the hall, the very picture of outraged respectability, with her bustle twitching pettishly behind her.

Peggy Earnshaw came into the hallway and stopped short when she saw Vic. "Hello, Vic," she said in her soft voice. "I didn't know you had come home."

In a year's time he had tried to forget Peg Earnshaw and there were times when he was sure he had succeeded, only to have the warm and lovely memory of her flood back into his body and soul. Her oval face and great grey eyes, her soft mouth and dark titian shair. She hadn't changed, in fact she seemed to be lovelier than ever. Somehow the mingled blood of the Earnshaws and the Dunlaps had amalgamated into Peggy Earnshaw, with all the finer features of both families. Mark Earnshaw had been a

25

ruggedly handsome man and his wife had been a local belle in her time.

She came towards him and all the old longing for her came back in a rush to Vic. He forgot the old quarrels they used to have, for both of them were high spirited and independent. He forgot how she had taken up with Dick Chapman to make him jealous, or so everyone had said. Vic had walked out on her then or so he had thought. He knew well enough now that he could never really walk out on Peggy Earnshaw. He took her by the arm and guided her into the living-room, with its prim overstuffed upholstery, marble-topped tables, elegant Argand and Rochester lamps, a Rogers Civil War group here and there, and antimacassars in plenty.

"What is wrong, Vic?" she asked. She eyed him closely.

Vic raised a hand and let it fall. He had never been able to hurt Peg Earnshaw and he had never before had a message that even approached the tragic news he must tell her this rainy night. "It's about your father and Buck," he said at last.

"Go on," she said steadily.

He looked up at her. "I came back by way of Skull Valley," he said at last. "Your father's house was burned to the ground.

The horses had been driven off. Not a soul was around."

"Where did you find them?" she asked quietly.

He looked at her quickly. "You know then?"

"I don't know anything that might have happened to them, Vic, I only know that I have been expecting something. Are they dead Vic? *Both* of them?"

"Yes, Peggy."

She turned away and walked to the fireplace, resting a hand on the mantel and her head on her hand. "Tell me," she said at last.

"I found them in the creek pass. Shot to death. Looks as though they never knew who killed them."

"Did you bring them in?"

"I'm going back for them now."

Her shoulders shook a little. "All of them," she said in a broken voice. "Big rugged Norman, quiet, steady Phillip, smiling Buck, and my father... It's too much, Vic."

"And Bennett Earnshaw, his two boys Nick and Saylor, Webb Dunlap as well. The blood debt is full to overflowing, Peggy."

"It wasn't worth it," she said.

"They wouldn't have lived any other way," he said.

"No."

Vic walked to the fireplace and rested a hand on her shoulder. "I'm sorry," he said.

"Why did you come back, Vic?"

"Jim Fancher sent for me."

"Is that all?"

Now was the chance to tell her, but it wasn't in Vic to say the words. He hadn't known she was still single and was back in Banister. Now was the time! Vic raised his head. "Jim was like a father to me," he said quietly. "Now that Little Mac is gone he wanted me to come back. Jim is scared, Peggy. He's getting old. Years ago he would have been a man to reckon with, but now he's just a frightened old man. He's been warned to keep his mouth shut. Jim always was a talker, but now it seems as though he's going too far. Now that Little Mac is gone, he has no one else to depend on but me. He always wanted me to stay at the ranch and take it over when he was gone. It looks like that might be the future for me now, Peg."

She turned and looked steadily at him. "If you're not killed too, Vic."

"I can take care of myself."

"So could my father and my uncle, my brothers and my cousins. Now all I have left

28

is Joe Dunlap. Joe is no fighter, Vic. You know that. Besides, he's taken to the bottle."

Vic nodded. "He always did like his likker."

"When will you bring them in, Vic?"

"Tonight."

"Let me know when you get here."

"I'll come myself."

She walked with him to the front door. He put on his slicker. "You'll sell the place now?" he asked.

"No," she said.

He stared at her. "You don't aim to keep it!"

Her eyes were as hard as glass when she looked at him. "Maybe you've forgotten I'm an Earnshaw too, Vic."

"This is loco! You can't run that place! You can't fight to keep it against whoever is working to clean out the Earnshaws! It's utter foolishness!"

"It's Earnshaw land, Vic. I'm the last of the Earnshaws. I'm going to move out there and *run that ranch.*"

Vic shrugged. "There speaks the fighting Earnshaw heart," he said. He opened the door and looked at her. "Think it over, Peg. Think it over..." He closed the door behind him and walked to his horse. The rain had stopped. He rolled a cigarette and mounted the grey. He lighted the smoke and glanced at the imposing wooden edifice erected by Amy Chapman, a fortress of respectability and good manners. He spat into the mud and spurred the grey back towards the centre of the town.

Three mounted men sat their horses in front of the Nevada Joy. One of them held the halter of a led horse. The led horse had a bundle of canvas on his back and two lanterns lashed atop the bundle. Forrie Cooke nodded to Vic as he rode up. "Figured we could use the led horse and one of ours to pull the buckboard."

"Good enough." Vic looked closely at the third man. "Hello, Joe," he said.

Joe Dunlap nodded. "Figured I better ride out with you boys when I heard the news." His speech was slurred and uneven. The ripe odour of whisky floated towards Vic. "Pretty damned bad, ain't it, Vic?"

Forrie Cooke kneed his horse next to that of Vic. "I told him to stay here until we got back. He won't listen to reason. He's pretty damned drunk, Vic."

Joe hiccupped. "I ain't lettin' old Vic Standish ride into that devil's canyon with you two hombres, without a real friend bein' with him. I got no use for you, Cooke, and you neither, Budd."

"Hear, hear," said Chuck Budd.

Vic was too tired and confused to argue with the drunken man. "Come on," he said. He spurred the grey and rode in the lead towards the bridge. As he rode he rolled another cigarette. He wasn't worried about Forrie Cooke. The man was too clever to ride out into the darkness with a man known to be a friend and ally of the Earnshaws, without figuring ahead what would happen to him if anything happened to Vic. The same thing could apply to Joe Dunlap. Maybe the killers didn't want to bother with Joe Dunlap. The Lazy E would go to Peggy Earnshaw. She was the one they'd have to deal with unless she changed her mind and sold out. Vic wasn't so sure Peggy would do that. As she had said: "It's Earnshaw land, Vic. I'm the last of the Earnshaws. I'm going to move out there and *run that ranch.*" They might bury her beside her blood kin on that same ranch if the pattern kept working out the way it had been up until this very day.

Chapter Three

The rain had stopped and a watery looking moon was peering through the gaps in the ragged drifting clouds over the mountains when Vic Standish and his three companions turned into the creek pass. Now and then the sound of a horseshoe striking a rock echoed through the pass. None of them spoke. It wasn't quite the place for needless conversation. The faint light of the moon was filtering down into the pass when at last Vic saw the buckboard ahead of them.

"This is a helluva place," growled Chuck Budd.

"But a good place for a drygulching," said Forrie Cooke.

"You ought'a know," said Joe Dunlap.

Vic turned in his saddle. "Keep your mouth shut, Joe," he said.

"You givin' the orders here, Standish? I can say what I like." Joe swallowed hard as he saw the hell look on Vic's tanned face. "Aright, aright," he grumbled. He felt inside his slicker and brought out a bottle. He drank deeply, then stowed the bottle away again.

"Thanks, Dunlap," said Chuck Budd drily.

Vic swung down from the grey and walked to the buckboard. The tarp had been soaked in the rain and it had sagged down upon the blue faces of the two dead men, outlining their profiles sharply. Vic pulled back the wet tarp. The bodies had not been disturbed. "Light those lanterns," he said.

Forrie Cooke lighted both lanters. By the light of them, they straightened out the two bodies and covered them with the tarp brought from town. All the time he was working, Vic was thinking. The buckboard had been headed to the north, towards the ranch, with Mark Earnshaw driving, and with Buck beside him, on his right. Mark had been shot through the right temple and Buck's lower jaw had been almost shot off by a slug striking it on the right side. That meant of course that the killer, or killers had fired from somewhere across the creek.

Chuck Budd was harnessing the led horse and his own horse to the rig. Joe Dunlap was leaning against a tree. Now and then the gurgling of the liquor in the bottle came to Vic. Forrie Cooke took out the makings and rolled a cigarette. He handed sack and papers to Vic. "Damned big slug hit Buck," he said quietly.

Vic nodded as he rolled a smoke. He accepted a light from the gunman. "It would take one helluva big slug to tear a man's jaw loose like that."

Cooke blew out a reflective puff of smoke. "It was a smaller calibre that killed Mark Earnshaw," he said.

"Easy enough," said Vic. "There must have been *two* drygulchers."

The blue eyes flicked across the rushing creek. "From over there."

"That's what I figure."

Cooke shoved back his hat. "The slugs came from up high," he said.

"Damned good shooting," said Chuck Budd.

"First-class-stuff," agreed Cooke.

Vic took his cigarette from his mouth. "They never knew what hit them."

"A helluva good place for a drygulching," said Chuck.

"They evidently knew just when the two Earnshaws were coming through here," said Forrie Cooke. He drew in deeply on his cigarette, then flipped it neatly into the water. He eyed Vic. "You want to take a look on the other side?"

"For what?" asked Vic. It was almost as though the man had read his mind, but Vic hadn't intended to look around up there in the company of men like Forrie Cooke and Chuck Budd. "The sheriff will probably do that."

"If we had a sheriff," said Forrie.

Vic looked quickly at him. "What do you mean?"

"Didn't Ben Cullen tell you?"

"Tell me what?"

Forrie smiled. "The sheriff was kicked out of office about a month ago for malfeasance. He got a sharp lawyer and raised ned about it. It hasn't been settled yet. You know this county was always a political hotbed. Well, the war is on again. Sheriff Cranmer says he's still sheriff, the county officials, for the most part, say he ain't. So meanwhile, until the thing gets settled, it's just like we had no sheriff at all."

"Malfeasance," said Chuck Budd. "What's that? Sounds dirty to me."

"No sheriff and no law you mean," said Vic quietly.

"That's about the size of it," agreed Forrie. He smiled. "Amusing, ain't it? And us *taxpayers* with two corpses on our hands."

Vic flipped his cigarette into the creek. "Let's take that look," he said. He mounted his grey and waited for Cooke to mount. The

35

two of them spurred their horses towards the stream.

There was a sudden outburst of orange-red flame high on the rugged escarpment wall that hemmed in the eastern side of the narrow pass. The lantern that stood on a rock two feet to one side of Joe Dunlap was lifted cleanly from its position and shattered as though struck by a mallet. Glass and burning oil splattered over the man. The heavy echo of the shot slammed back and forth between the narrow walls of the pass and fled off.

Vic hit the ground and bellied through the chilly mud to a big boulder. Forrie Cooke had spurred his horse behind a high rock ledge. Chuck Budd had swept the second lantern from the tailgate of the buckboard as he dived for cover. Joe Dunlap screamed as he slapped out the flames that were licking at his wet slicker. He rolled over a rock and lay flat.

The echo died away. There was no sound in the pass except the steady, rushing murmur of the rain swollen creek. Vic slowly raised his head, removing his hat as he did so. He kept a clump of scraggly brush between him and the unseen marksman. The escarpment was dark except for the very top of it, which was limned softly by the silvery

36

moonlight. There was no sight nor sound of anyone up there.

Forrie Cooke dismounted and took his Winchester from its sheath. Vic stood up behind his boulder and slowly lowered his hand to his Colt. He wanted no part of Forrie Cooke standing behind him with a cocked rifle in his more than capable hands.

"Turn the team around, Chuck," said Forrie.

"Keno," said the big man. He kept the team between himself and the hidden marksman as he turned it.

"Now lead it behind that rock shoulder there," said Forrie.

Chuck led team and buckboard out of sight. Forrie walked over to where Joe Dunlap was hiding. "Get up," he said.

"You go to hell! That shot was meant for me!"

"He missed, didn't he? Get up, or by God, I'll do the job he messed up!" Forrie poked the man with the muzzle of the rifle.

Vic got his horse and led it towards the two men. "I'll take care of him, Forrie," he said.

The man turned and grinned. "What's the matter, Standish, don't you trust me?"

"He killed Norm," mumbled Joe.

Cooke shrugged. He led his horse along the road until he too was out of sight.

Vic pulled Joe to his feet and reached inside the man's slicker. He pulled out the bottle and shoved the man towards the others. He led both horses slowly along the road, keeping them between him and that eagle-eyed marksman on the heights.

The three of them looked at him as he rounded a rock shoulder. "Who do you think it was?" asked Chuck Budd.

"How should I know?" snapped Vic. "I'm new here. You hombres are more used to what's going on around this country than I am." Vic took out the bottle. He handed it to Chuck.

The big man shook the bottle. "Don't take a helluva lot to get Joe drunk," he said with a grin. He drank deeply.

"You forget he's probably been swilling the stuff all day," said Forrie.

"Go to hell," growled Joe.

Chuck handed the bottle back to Vic. Vic looked at Forrie.

"No thanks," said Forrie, "I'm a teetotaler. Surprised, Standish?"

Vic raised the bottle. "It doesn't surprise me," he said. "Gives a man an edge sometimes."

"What do you mean by that?" asked Forrie coldly.

Vic drank. He lowered the bottle, feeling

38

the hotness and life of the rye running into his body. "More than one drunk has been killed by a gunman who was cold sober. Adds to the notches, and no questions asked."

"You mean like Norm Earnshaw?"

There was a sudden tenseness amongst the four men.

Forrie Cooke spoke quietly. "He was as sober as I am now, Standish."

"Yeh, yeh," said Joe Dunlap.

Chuck Budd withdrew his rifle from its saddle scabbard and turned towards Vic. "Feel better in this hellhole with a gun in my hands."

Vic felt cold all over despite the sudden warmth of the rye he had swallowed. Forrie Cooke still had his Winchester in his hand. Joe Dunlap was swaying back and forth. He gripped his saddle to steady himself.

"I had a feeling you'd throw up that Earnshaw killing to me sooner or later," said Forrie. "That's why I volunteered to come along and give you a hand."

"Hawww!" said Joe. "You two! You kill me! Two Earnshaw killers trying to act like public spirited citizens. By God, I'm almost glad I'm drunk."

Vic glanced at him. "What do you mean by *two* Earnshaw killers, Joe?" he asked.

39

Joe peered blearily at him. "Didn' you know who killed Nick in a barroom brawl here some time ago?"

An icy fist seemed to close on Vic's guts. He looked directly at Chuck Budd. The man's eyes seemed to be as hard and as flat as stone. "Yeh," said Budd. "It was me done the job, Standish. Nick started it and I finished it."

There was no chance for Vic to make a break. He cursed himself for being drawn into this trap. Both men were experts in the art of killing. Fair or foul, they were both experts, and Joe Dunlap was worse than useless now. Both Joe and Vic could be dropped in the mud with .44/40 slugs in their guts. Joe Dunlap was the last of the men of the Earnshaw clan, as poor a specimen as he was.

One of the horses whinnied. Then another took it up. Forrie Cooke glanced up towards the escarpment. "Let's haul tail out'a here," he said. "That sonofabitch might just be stalking us." He let down the hammer of his rifle to half cock and swung up onto his horse, placing the rifle across his thighs. Chuck Budd climbed heavily into the buckboard and threaded the reins through his thick and powerful fingers. He slapped the reins on the backs of the horses and drove to the south followed by Forrie Cooke.

Vic's throat was brassy dry and his guts were churning. He took another drink, then mounted the grey. "Come on, Joe," he said quietly. He rode after the buckboard.

The valley of Piney Creek was flooded with moonlight when the party emerged from the haunted pass. None of them spoke as they turned left on the road that led to Banister. Now and then Vic would look back over his shoulder towards the brooding hills that overlooked the pass and beyond the pass the lonely and silent Valley of the Skull. A fitting name for the place. Death was more at home there than life.

"She'll have to sell now," said Joe at last.

Vic looked at the drunken man. "Peggy?" he asked.

"Yeh. It's been too much for me, Vic. Sure, I'm supposed to be one of the fightin' Earnshaws, and as long as I could ride with fighters who laid the chunk like Norm, and Phil, and Buck, it was all right. But they been whittled away, Vic, whittled away until there ain't no one left but me and Peg. I been scared for years now. The bottle ain't the answer, you might say, but it's the only way I know to keep from lying awake every night wondering when it's going to come to me."

Joe shivered. He took the bottle from Vic's hand. He drank deeply and handed it back. "Thanks. You saw how close that shot come tonight, Vic."

"He missed," said Vic drily.

"No, he hit what he wanted to hit, Vic! He could'a hit me just as easy as that lantern, Vic. It was a warning."

"You're drunk."

"No," said Joe. He solemnly waggled his head. "Look, Vic: He killed Buck and Mark, didn' he?"

"Maybe."

"He did! How far would you say that shot was fired from tonight?"

"Two hundred yards, Joe."

"Two hundred? More like four or five hundred! At night, Vic! downhill! Could you hit that lantern under those conditions?"

"I doubt it," said Vic.

Joe looked ahead at the others. Forrie Cooke was riding close beside the buckboard talking to Chuck. "It was Forrie Cooke lighted them lanterns. It was him that put it on the rock right next to me, Vic. He marked me, Vic. I swear he did!"

Vic rubbed his bristly jaw. He was tireder than ever. It was getting harder and harder to think and the little rye he had imbibed wasn't helping too much.

42

"The next time he shoots at me, Vic, he won't miss. When I'm gone, that leaves Peg. Maybe they won't kill a woman, but I wouldn't put it past them. You tell her she ought'a sell that damned place. It ain't worth even killing me, Vic."

"And no law in the country," said Vic. "At least none that can be relied upon."

"Funny thing Ben Cullen didn't tell you about Sheriff Cranmer."

"Yeh," said Vic softly.

"And if we don't have an investigation by the county it looks like we'll have to bury Mark and Buck without ever finding out who done them in."

Vic turned in his saddle again. "Maybe," he said.

"You keep out of this thing, Vic. Peg still has a soft spot in her pretty head for you. If she sells the Lazy E she'll have a damned fine dowry for some lucky man, Vic."

"Shut up, Joe! You always did talk too much!"

"I was only trying to think of a way out of this mess!"

"Then keep it to yourself!"

Vic spurred forward.

"Leave the jug with me," said Joe.

Vic took a drink and then heaved the bottle across a ditch. It shattered against a rock.

43

"Go lap it up, you drunken bastard," he shot back over his shoulder.

They clattered over the log bridge just as the moon vanished behind the ragged clouds. A cold wind blew up the valley and banged the store signs along the main street of Banister. There seemed to be a warning in the moaning voice of the wind. A warning to Vic Standish to get out of that country while he was still alive.

Chapter Four

They had buried Mark Earnshaw and his youngest son in the family cemetery on the knoll overlooking the creek. The sun was bright in the heavens that day. It had been shining fully for two days, drying out the wetness of the rain that had swept across the country and filled the waterholes and streams. When the burial was over, the people who had come from far and wide to pay their respects to almost the last of the Earnshaws left a little hurriedly. Skull Valley, even in the bright sunlight of that sad day, was no longer a place where one would linger if he didn't have to stay.

Jim Fancher leaned against the cemetery fence watching the buckboards and spring wagons flowing south and north along the valley road. "Good people," he said to Vic Standish. "But somehow I had the feeling that some of them seemed almost glad that the last of the fighting Earnshaws was gone. There was an awful lot of fighting and bloodshed in their day, Vic. Maybe the good Lord figured there had been too much of it and finally settled the whole thing in His way."

"You mean He condoned coldblooded murder to settle it?" said Vic shortly.

Jim shrugged. "The Lord works in devious ways," he said. He shook his head. "Too bad. Well, the ranch ain't on a par with mine, Vic, but it's still good land. Peggy should get a good price for it."

Vic rolled a cigarette and lighted it. He looked down to where the Earnshaw house had stood, now marked by a flattened bed of ashes and rusting iron. The warm wind fluttered skirts down there. Peggy Earnshaw was standing there with Amy Chapman and Joe Dunlap. There was another man there. Tall Dick Chapman. It was him who had driven his aunt and Peggy Earnshaw out from Banister.

"Yes, sir," said Jim. "By Godfrey, Vic, if

45

you were interested in ranching, I'd make an offer for the place myself. With this place and mine we'd be able to make a cattle empire."

Vic glanced at him. "You told me the first night I came back that you and Little Mac had been hoping you'd get an offer for your place. You haven't got enough cattle on your place to keep a goatherd busy. I thought you wanted out of ranching, Jim."

The older man smiled. "That was before you came back, Vic. With you here I feel better. Hellsfire, Vic! When I pass on the whole of everything I own goes to you. I've got a few productive years left and I can work with you to see you get started on your way to be a man of substance."

"What about all the warnings you received? You think they, whoever *they* are, will sit back and let you and me run this place when they've already just about wiped out the Earnshaws to get their hands on the Lazy E? You don't make sense, Jim."

Jim nodded. "Yeh," he said wearily. "Well, it was a dream. Since Little Mac passed on, boy, I haven't been able to think at all clearly."

"Besides, Peg means to ranch here, Jim."

Jim Fancher's lower jaw dropped. "You're joshing me, Vic!"

46

"No, Jim. She has made up her mind."

"That's loco! A woman running this place! She's got no men kin! No cowpokes would want to work for this spread after all the shooting that's been going on here!"

Vic blew out a smoke ring. "I've been over all that with her already, Jim."

"By God, I'll talk to her myself!" Jim stalked off down the slope, the very picture of outraged manhood. Vic couldn't help but grin. He wished in his heart that Jim was ten or fifteen years younger. The old man had been a fighter in times past.

Vic looked at the freshly mounded graves. He looked at the others, by now smoothly grass grown, and he remembered the Earnshaws and the Dunlaps he had known and ridden knee to knee with in the old days. That grass was nurtured by some of the best fighting blood in Nevada. He looked down the long valley, bright in the sunlight. Maybe it had been worth it. Vic could be no judge of that, for he was not a man who loved the land as a farmer or rancher loved it. The country he loved well enough. Far more than he would admit even to himself.

He rolled another cigarette and looked across the bright waters of the stream to the rugged wall of the dark escarpment and to the looming rock formation that seemed always to cast a chill of brooding fear over the valley. The sun was striking it in such a way that the great eyeholes seemed to be looking down at him with a speculative look. "You're next, Standish," they seemed to flash the silent message to him."

Vic spat. "Go take a flying leap at the moon," he said, but he could not cast the chill from his soul.

He walked down the long slope to where the others stood talking. Dick Chapman turned a little as he saw Vic. There had never been much love lost between them even in the days before Dick had laid suit to Peggy Earnshaw. Dick was tall and Dick was goodlooking, but Dick didn't like work. Dick liked the poker tables of Banister and rumour had it that his aunt had sent him off east for an education some years ago to keep him away from Mineral Street and the doxies that abided there. But Dick Chapman always seemed to have money in his pockets, the best of horses, the finest of clothing, and whether or not he got it from his doting aunt was never quite clear to the good people of Banister. Before Vic Standish had left the area Dick had seemed to settle down a little, to study law it was said, under the guidance of old Judge Tecumseh Porter. This had given handsome Dick an air of respectability, and the future of a man of parts, and nothing had been more pleasing to Amy Chapman.

Jim Fancher was waving his long arms as he talked to Peggy Earnshaw. Joe Dunlap stood to one side with the haggard look of the perennial drunk who is just waiting for the opportunity to get out of sight long enough to get a good belt from his hidden bottle. He had been drunk ever since he had returned to Banister with Vic, Forrie Cooke and Chuck Budd the night before last. Vic had been surprised that he had been able to gird his loins enough to make the funeral.

The look from Amy Chapman's eye was enough to stop any ordinry man, but it glanced off Vic like a pea from the shell of a desert tortoise. Vic leaned against a tree, half listening to Jim's pleas with Peggy. From the set of her straight back and shoulders, Vic knew well enough that Jim could save his breath.

Dick Chapman sauntered over to Vic. "Haven't had a chance to talk with you, Standish," he said in his smooth voice. "I was quite surprised to learn you had returned."

"Like a bad penny, eh, Chapman?"

Dick smiled. "Still sore because I cut you out with Peggy?"

Vic shrugged. "It's her business, Chapman."

The dark eyes were speculative as the taller man studied Vic. "No hard feelings, eh?"

"None." Vic waved a careless hand.

"Must have been quite a blow to you. You always rated pretty high with the young maidens of Banister."

Vic felt for the makings. "Like you rate with the whores on Mineral Street, eh?"

The man flushed. He glanced quickly at the others. "That's no way to talk in front of ladies!"

"They couldn't hear me, what with Jim talking at the top of his voice."

Chapman lighted a cigar. "Seems odd that you should suddenly show up after a year on the very day Mark and Buck Earnshaw get drygulched."

A big hand shot out and gripped the wrist of the hand that had lighted the cigar. Dick Chapman winced at the steel-like strength in that hand as it pulled the match holding hand to the cigarette Vic had just fashioned. Vic's hard eyes peered through the smoke and it seemed to Dick Chapman that they were the eyes of a devil looking out of a smokey window of hell itself. "What exactly do you mean by that, Chapman?" asked Vic.

Chapman swallowed hard. He pulled back his hand but could not release it from Vic's grasp. "I was just commenting on the coincidence," he said quickly.

Vic released the hand. "You do a little thinking the next time before you make a comment like that," he said coldly.

There was pure hate in Dick's eyes. He could handle a gun with some of the best of them and wasn't lacking in a form of courage, but Vic Standish was like a hunting lobo and he could strike like a diamondback when the need arose. "Just stay away from Peg," he said thinly.

"That's up to her, isn't it?"

"You ran off to God knows where, didn't you? She was engaged to me before you even left."

Vic smiled a crooked smile. "Long engagement, isn't it, Chappie?"

"That's our business."

Vic eyed him speculatively. "Now that Peg is the last of the Earnshaws maybe you figure on moving in to get your paws into the money if she sells the ranch. I wouldn't put it past you."

The man swung so fast that Vic had hardly time to block the blow with his left forearm. He slammed a right cross to Chapman's smoothly shaven jaw. The man went down hard and seemed to bounce a little as he hit the ground. His right hand darted inside his coat. Vic stepped in close and kicked out with his right foot, striking the little double-barrelled derringer from Chapman's hand even as it exploded. The slug whined thinly right over the heads of the trio near the site of the burned house. Joe Dunlap hit the ground and crawled behind a tree. Amy Chapman clutched her bonnet and screamed shrilly.

Vic stepped back. "Get up," he said thinly.

Dick got slowly to his feet.

"Put up your fists," said Vic.

"Not here, Vic," said Jim Fancher.

Vic nodded. He walked over and picked up the derringer. It was a lovely thing, as deadly as it was. The barrels were chased with silver and the butt plates were finely carved. Vic emptied the loaded chamber. Dick held out his hand for the gun. Vic turned and threw the little gun with all his strength towards the creek. It splashed into the middle of the stream. It was almost a childish thing to do but there was no reasoning with Vic Standish in the mood he was in. "The next time you pull a gun on me, Chapman," he said quietly, "I'll kill you." He walked to his horse and mounted it, spurring towards the road.

The pass road was empty of life. Vic rode to the place where he had found the buckboard with the bodies of the two Earnshaws. On an impulse he swam the horse across the creek and rode into the quiet, dark woods that bordered the creek and filled the bottomland between it and the sheer wall of the escarpment that towered above the pass. He dismounted when he reached the rock wall and looked up at it. An agile man could make his way up that wall without too much trouble. He pulled off his spurs, took his lariat and started up the rock face. It was fairly easy going until he was three quarters of the way up, and then he realized he could hardly go further as the rock face was sheer and smooth. He squatted on a ledge and rolled a cigarette, eyeing the creek far below him, the rutted road, and the pass to right and left of him. It was a real bird's eye view of the rugged terrain. He could even see part of the Lazy E spread and beyond it, to his right, and almost in line with his position, the grinning skull formation.

He looked about the ledge on which he rested. It was almost like a cut-away path made by nature for man's convenience.

He walked towards the area where he remembered seeing the gun flash the night the hidden marksman had shattered the lantern beside Joe Dunlap. He reached the approximate area and looked about. There was no earth on the ledge to reveal boot tracks. He looked down and saw the rock shoulder where he and the others had taken shelter the night they had removed the bodies from the pass road. Then he scanned along the road until he could identify the tree and rock in the area where Joe had been standing. He was standing in just about the spot where the marksman had fired from as far as he could estimate.

The wind moaned softly down the sunlit pass. The trees swayed and thrashed. A lone hawk hung almost motionless in the air current high above the great gash in the rocky earth. Vic looked back and forth. Nothing. He rolled another cigarette and lighted it, blowing the smoke out into the pass, watching the wind ravel it and carry it away. He looked down and as he did so something glinted brassily from ten feet below the ledge. He dropped on to his lean belly and looked down. It was a spent cartridge case wedged between a scrub tree and the rock face in a pocket of shallow earth.

Vic flipped away the cigarette and uncoiled his lariat. He looped it about a smooth boulder, pulled off his boots, then let himself down the rock face until he could pick up the empty hull. He pocketed it and pulled himself easily up to the ledge. He squatted and took the cartridge case from his pocket. It was a big hull and it hadn't been lying out in the weather long enough to be dulled by corrosion. He turned it and studied the base of it. The case was over three inches long and it must carry a whopping charge and a huge bullet. "Big Fifty Sharps," said Vic. He remembered the wound that had caused Buck Earnshaw's death. Forrie Cooke had mentioned that it would have taken one helluva big slug to tear a man's lower jaw almost completely off from the range the gun had been fired at from across the creek. The Big Fifty Sharps could do it for the 170 grain powder charge drove a massive 700 grain slug. The base of the cartridge was marked U.M.C. for Union Metallic Cartridge Company, as well as the calibre.

Vic hefted the empty hull in his hand. The autopsy held in Banister by Doc Parch had showed that the slug that had killed Mark Earnshaw had been a common calibre used in that country, the .44/40 which was interchangeable between rifle and pistol, thus

55

saving the trouble of carrying separate cartridges for each of the weapons. The slug that had caused Buck's death wound had evidently torn the man's jaw almost off in passage,then had gone on to bury itself in the ground or into a tree, but there had been speculation in Vic's mind that it would have taken more than a .44/40 bullet to do the horrible job.

Vic looked down into the pass. Joe Dunlap had argued that the marksman who had shot at him had fired from a range of four or five hundred yards. The drunk had been right at that. Vic shook his head. Firing at night, downhill, as the marksman had done the night he had shattered the lantern would have taken the skill of a top sharpshooter. The puzzling factor was that both Earnshaws must have been fired at from about where Vic was now situated and from the fact that two different rifles had been used, both killers had been about equal in skill, and the odds were in Vic's mind that the man who had fired the .44/40 must have been the better of the two. Vic himself was pretty good with the long gun, and he knew well enough in his own mind that he could never have hit a target a small as a man's head at that range with his own .44/40 Winchester saddle gun, and he would have been hard put to do it with the extremely accurate and powerful Sharps Big Fifty, a long range weapon hardly with a peer in either American or European manufacture.

Vic walked back to where he had ascended the rock face, and let himself down slowly and carefully. Now and then rock fragments would break off and fall far below him. He breathed a lot easier when he reached the firm ground. He mounted the dun and recrossed the creek. As he reached the far side he saw the area where the Earnshaws had died. He ground reined the dun and poked about in the brush and rock behind the place where he had come across the buckboard. He whistled softly as he saw a splotch of brightness on a rock and beside it the flattened shape of a big lead slug. He pried it from the rock with his pocketknife. The base of it, where it was fitted into the mouth of the cartridge case gave no doubt but what it was a Sharps Big Fifty. He dropped it into his shirt pocket and walked back to his horse. All he had to do now was to find a man who could fire the big accurate weapon with the skill to kill a man at five hundred yards downhill, and to shatter a lantern at night at the approximate same range. Maybe Joe Dunlap was right at that. The drunk had said the hidden marksman had hit what he had *wanted* to hit. The lantern and not Joe Dunlap. It *had* been a warning.

Vic mounted his dun and rode south. The warm sun dried the hide of his horse and his wet trousers so that by the time he reached Piney Creek he was thoroughly dry.

There was no law in the country, at least none that was functioning. No law to find the man, or men who had murdered two of the finest men Vic had ever known. By the time the question as to who was the legal representative of the law in the country was settled, the killers would have covered their tracks. There was one man, and one man alone who would not let the murderers rest. Vic Standish had made up his mind. Jim Fancher was afraid of the hidden killers. Joe Dunlap feared them as well. Peggy Earnshaw would die by the hands of the unknown killers if she persisted in running the Lazy E. Vic rolled a cigarette and rode slowly towards Fancher's place. It was a good spread, one of the best in that country, but Jim was hardly running it as a paying proposition now. The number of head he had was hardly enough to call the place a cattle ranch. He didn't even have hands living at the home place, just a few out on the range, riding fence and keeping an eye on the stock.

In the days when Little Mac had been alive it had been quite different, but then Little Mac had been the real rancher of the two, though Jim Fancher had been a good balance wheel for the somewhat volatile and excitable Canadian Scot.

All Vic had to do was to agree to work with Jim to ranch, possibly to take over the Lazy E range as well, and his future, in a business sense, would be assured. Vic felt the empty cartridge case and the mutilated slug bumping gently against his chest as he rode. He might be assured of something else as well; *a Sharps Big Fifty through his thick head.*

Chapter Five

It was dusk of a warm evening when Vic Standish rode across the bridge spanning the river and rode along the main street of Banister. He dismounted in front of the marshal's office and walked into the smokey interior. Ben Cullen was seated at his roll top desk, big feet planted amidst the litter of papers atop it, cigar thrust upward at an angle from his mouth and a wraith of tobacco smoke rifting about his head. "Evenin', Vic," he said. "Fill up a cuppa coffee, amigo."

Vic filled a granite cup and sat down on a chair. He tilted it back against the wall. "They buried Mark and Buck Earnshaw today, Ben."

"I ought'a know," said the marshal.

"What are you going to do about it?"

"What can I do? I got no jurisdiction outside of Banister. It's the sheriff's job, Vic. You know that. You been a deputy yourself."

"Never in a county like this one."

"Oh, it ain't so bad."

Vic sipped his coffee. "It looks to me like no one is much concerned about that double murder, Ben."

"Now that ain't so! I liked both of them men. Everybody did! Mark Earnshaw was a hard man, but likeable as hell! Buck, well, you was Buck's amigo for years. Everybody liked Buck."

"Everybody but the man who drygulched him, Ben."

Ben dropped his feet and swivelled his chair. "Look, Vic," he said quietly, "you've been away for quite a spell. This isn't your fight. Sure, you was good friends with the Earnshaws, but that was in the days when they were a power in this county. Well, you know where most of them are now. It'd be best for you to stick with Jim Fancher and keep your nose out of this mess."

"Supposing I don't?"

Ben took the cigar from his mouth. "You're too young to die, Vic."

"What's Jason Kile got to do with all this killing?"

Ben Cullen's eyes narrowed. "Who mentioned him in connection with these killings?"

"Never mind."

"It was Jim Fancher, wasn't it?"

"Maybe."

"You know damned well it was! Jim has no use for Kile and his so-called combine."

"Is there such a thing?"

Ben relighted his cigar.

"Ben?"

Ben waved out the match flame and dropped the match into the garboon. "Jason Kile is a businessman, Vic. He's got his fingers into a lot of deals. He's a hard man, Vic."

"Like he was down in the Pioche country."

Ben leaned back and studied Vic through the wreathing tobacco smoke. "Vic," he said softly, "I warned you that this wasn't your fight. You fool around with Jason Kile, and happen to mention Pioche to him and I wouldn't give a plugged nickle for you."

"Meaning he'd have me killed?"

Ben shook his head. "No, but he'd give you the damnedest hurrahing you ever had, and no one would ever pin a shred of guilt on him. He's too smart for that."

"We'll see about that," said Vic drily. He leaned forward and handed Ben the empty cartridge case and the mutilated slug he had found in the pass. "Ever see one like that, Ben?"

The marshall pursed his lips. "Sharps Big Fifty, I'd say." He looked at Vic. "Where did you pick these up?"

"In the pass where Mark and Buck Earnshaw were killed."

"So?"

"The night we went for the bodies someone shot at Joe Dunlap, or at least close enough to him to scare him into a two days' drunk."

"Yeh, Forrie Cooke told me about that." Ben leaned back in his chair. "What do you think?"

"It took a long range rifle, fired by a top marksman to kill Buck Earnshaw, and another one to kill Mark Earnshaw. It took a man with the same skill and the same type of accurate weapon to shoot out that lantern beside Joe."

"Go on."

Vic rolled a cigarette. "Who do you know around here who can shoot like that?"

"Plenty of men, Vic. You for instance."

"I'm not that good, Ben."

Ben rubbed his jaw. "Anyone else know you picked these up?"

"No."

"Keep this to yourself. I'll do a little investigating about it."

"Any news from the sheriff?"

"No. The line has been repaired. I sent a wire in this morning about the killings. No answer as yet."

"Send another."

Vic stood up and took the cartridge case and slug from Ben's hand. "Why does Jason Kile want to buy the Lazy E?"

"How should I know? He buys and sells all kinds of business."

"Good businesses?"

Ben looked up. "Certainly! I told you he was a good businessman."

"The Lazy E is a good spread, Ben, but there are better spreads around here. Like Jim Fancher's F Bar M. Kile never made Jim an offer."

"Maybe he doesn't want the F Bar M."

Vic walked to the door. "Then why would he want the Lazy E?"

Ben shrugged. "That's his business."

"Maybe it's my business too."

Ben shook his head. "I told you not to fool around with Jason Kile."

"Where can I find him?"

"His office is in the Mifflin Building, but during the evenings you can usually find him in the Banister House Bar, right next to the Mifflin Building. He owns the bar, Vic."

"I know where it is." Vic closed the door behind him.

Ben Cullen got up and walked to the window. He peered through the dirty streaked glass, watching Vic walk up the street. He shrugged, lighted another cigar, then clapped on his hat and hurried across the street towards the Banister House Bar, glancing over his shoulder as he did so to see Vic Standish enter Smiley's Gun Shop at the far end of the street.

It was fully dark when Vic left the gun shop. The moon had not yet arisen and only the lights from the store and shop windows illuminated Main Street, for the few street lamps of Banister hardly were able to dispel the darkness. His visit to the gun shop had been of no help. Jack Smiley had told Vic he hadn't sold a box of Sharps Big Fifty

64

cartridges in the past two or three years that he could remember. It wasn't a common calibre in that country. Now back in the buffalfo hunting country you could find any number of Sharps in various heavy calibres, but not in that part of Nevada at any rate. The findings of the empty cartridge case and the smashed slug was about as tenuous a clue as any investigator had ever faced. Still, somewhere in the Banister area there was a man, a deadly marksman, who had just such a rifle, and Vic was sure that when he found that man he would know who had murdered Mark and Buck Earnshaw.

Vic walked towards the Banister House Bar. He was curious about Jason Kile. He had never met Kile but he had heard aplenty about him long before Vic had returned to Banister. Kile's reputation had been bad enough around Pioche. According to Jim Fancher it was no better around Banister. Jim had also insisted that Forrie Cooke, a hired gun, had been put up to killing Norm Earnshaw in the streets of Banister. Chuck Budd had killed Nick Earnshaw in a barroom brawl. That must have been quite a fight, for Nick Earnshaw, of all the Earnshaw men, was the best rough and tumble artist of the lot in a family that could handle its fists as

65

well as its guns. Both Cooke and Budd were on Kile's payroll.

The Banister House Bar was full of early evening drinkers, local merchants having a few short ones before going home, ranchers who had been in town on business taking on a few for the road and meditating on staying on for the evening, regulars getting set for the long hours of drinking. There were a few women in the rear booths. They weren't allowed to stand up at the mahogany and ply their trade. The Banister House Bar was still the top level for them. After that they skidded down to the Nevada Joy and places of that ilk, then later descended to Mineral Street, before the long downward trail to oblivion and the filthy cribs of the Border towns.

Vic found a place at the end of the bar and ordered rye. Many of the men knew him by past acquaintance or reputation. At the far end of the bar was Forrie Cooke. He nodded as he saw Vic. There was rarely an expression on the gunman's face. His features were like a skilfully carved mask of brown wood. Even his blue eyes were hard and flat, but they were always moving, flicking back and forth, watchful and ready.

Ken Brucker, a lawyer, stood beside Vic.

66

"Let me buy you a drink, Standish," he said.

"I'm on." Vic had always liked the young lawyer. He had once been thought of as a likely successor to old Judge Porter until he had begun to spend more time with John Barleycorn than with Blackwell. "Ken," he said, "which one is Jason Kile?"

"The man in the grey suit in the end booth back there. The one with the papers on the table."

"And the young filly seated beside him?"

Ken grinned. "Yes. Jason Kile likes them young, Vic. But, what the hell, he pays well for their services."

Vic eyed the businessman. Kile was medium sized, dark of hair, with the sides of it distinguished by greying. His neatly trimmed moustache was also peppered and salted with grey. "What kind of man is he, Ken?"

"Hard as a diamond, Vic. No heart and all head. Not a man to fool with."

"In what way?"

The lawyer turned and studied Vic. "*Any way*, my friend. They say he has killed three men."

"Himself?"

"*Himself.*"

And how many has he *had* killed?"

67

Brucker paled. "For God's sake, Vic, don't talk like that!"

"Why? He has Forrie Cooke and Chuck Budd working for him, hasn't he? He wants to buy the Lazy E. The fighting Earnshaws were in his way. Now the only Earnshaws left are a woman and a drunk."

Ken looked nervously to one side and then the other. "I guess you're talking about Cooke killing Norm Earnshaw and Budd killing Nick Earnshaw."

"I am."

The lawyer downed his drink and refilled his glass.

"From all I know, Cooke shot down Earnshaw in a fair fight."

"*How* fair?"

"Well, Norm was no slouch with a six-gun, Vic."

"Was he drunk?"

"No."

"How did Cooke get away with it?"

"It was selfdefence according to the coroner's verdict, Vic. A fair enough shake from all the evidence."

"What about Nick?"

Ken studied the amber liquid in his glass. "I was there the night Nick was killed. His head struck a spike that was sticking out of the wall. Killed him as though he had been shot through the back of the head."

"How well was he holding up against Budd?"

"They tell me he was doing pretty well. Nick was a handy man with his fists."

"What do you mean? You were there. Weren't you sure about it?"

Brucker flushed. "I was pretty drunk, Vic. No one else seemed to think it was a rigged fight if that is what you're driving at."

"Selfdefence again? Coroner's verdict?"

"Yes."

"Very neat."

Ken filled Vic's glass. "Vic, for your own good, don't talk like that around Banister. Neither Cooke nor Budd like it hinted that both killings were planned. Sure, I know you can handle your guns and your fists, and maybe you could outdraw the one and outfight the other, but the odds are against it. *One* of them would get you in the end."

A man tapped Vic on the shoulder. "Standish," he said, "Mister Kile wants to see you."

"I'm right here, Mister." Vic turned and looked at the man, and if he had ever seen a hard case in his life, he knew he was looking into the metallic eyes of one right that very moment.

69

"I said he wanted to see you, Standish," repeated the man.

Brucker pressed a foot down on Vic's right foot. The message was plain enough. Vic downed his drink. "All right," he said.

The man smiled mechanically. "That's better, mister."

Vic nodded to Ken Brucker and walked through the crowded room to where Kile sat in his booth. Kile looked up. "Standish?" he asked.

"Yes."

"Sit down." Kile looked at the girl. "Get lost, Sadie." The girl flounced out of the booth and walked up the stairs leading to the second floor balcony, revealing a fine expanse of trim ankle and calf to anyone who might be interested. There were plenty of men interested, but they all knew whose property *she* was.

Kile's small eyes flicked up at Vic. "I asked you to sit down. It wasn't an order, Standish." A cold smile played about his mouth. "They say that no one gives orders to Vic Standish."

Vic sat down and eyed the man. "I learned to take orders when I was a kid, Mister Kile. From the right people, that is."

"Don't get the idea in your skull that I'm

trying to run Banister. I know these people better than that."

"You seem to be doing all right."

Kile shrugged. He pushed a silver cigar case towards Vic. "Light up. I want to talk to you."

Vic selected a cigar and lighted it. He poured himself a drink from the bottle on the table. "Shoot," he said comfortably.

Kile leaned back. "I know you are an old friend to the Earnshaw family, Standish. For that reason, I'd like you to do me a favour."

"Go on."

"Peggy Earnshaw refuses to sell the Lazy E."

"That's her business."

"So it is. I want that ranch."

"She won't sell."

Kile nodded. "I talked to her cousin, Joe Dunlap, who happens to have been left a small share of the place. He has agreed to sell out, but he can't sell out unless she agrees to do so too."

"And you want me to convince her?"

Kile smiled. "That's the idea."

"What's in it for me?"

The expression changed and became crafty. "We'll talk about that when we have something solid to stand upon."

"Why bother with the Lazy E? Jim

Fancher might be interested in selling the F
Bar M at the right price."

"So?"

"It's a far better piece of property than the
Lazy E, Kile. Any good businessman could
tell you that."

"It so happens I'm not interested in the
F Bar M, Standish."

Vic blew out a puff of smoke, then sipped
his drink. It was excellent brandy. "Would
you mind telling me why you're so interested
in the Lazy E, Kile?" he asked.

"Yes, I would mind," replied Kile.

Vic happened to look up. Forrie Cooke
was standing at the end of the bar. He had
been joined by Chuck Budd. The man who
had told Vic that Jason Kile wanted
to see him was behind Vic, near the
wall, seated in a chair, ostensibly watching
a poker game, but watching Vic even more
than the game. Vic wondered how many
other men in that crowd were on the Kile
payroll.

"Well, Standish?" asked Kile.

"I'll see what she says."

Kile nodded. "One other thing before you
leave. There has been a lot of talk going on
around here that I'm behind the bloodshed
that has been flowing about these past few
months. That I put Forrie Cooke up to

killing Norm Earnshaw and Chuck Budd up to killing Nick Earnshaw."

"So?"

Kile leaned forward. "They say Jim Fancher practically raised you. Is that right?"

"My mother died of fever when we first arrived in Nevada. My father was thrown and killed. Jim took me in when I was fourteen years old. I worked off and on for him up until about a year ago. Yes, you might say that he practically raised me."

Kile smiled. "Then you had better tell Mister Fancher that he has a big mouth. That he is constantly making insinuations, if not outright accusations that I am behind all these Earnshaw killings. You might also tell him, that if he persists in those insinuations, that I will have him charged with defamation of character. Is that clear?"

Vic stood up and nodded. "Very clear. Why don't you tell him yourself?"

"I have, Mister Standish, I have, but he is a very stubborn old man. Now you tell him what I have told you."

Vic smiled coldly. "You can tell him yourself, Kile. Now I'm going to tell *you* something. I don't like you and your high pressure methods; your hired gunslicks and your thugs. I don't like your approaching me

73

to pressure Peg Earnshaw into selling the Lazy E."

Kile waved a hand. Forrie Cooke and Chuck Budd moved towards the booth. "Take it easy, Mister Standish," said Kile, "or I may have to have you taught a lesson."

There was a cold flame within Vic Standish. He glanced up to see Chuck Budd pushing aside a chair. "Anything wrong, Mister Kile?" the big man said.

"Mister Standish is threatening me, Chuck. Escort him outside and warn him that I don't like to be threatened by him or anyone else around Banister."

Chuck Budd made the mistake of reaching out for Vic. Vic swung from the hip with a left that cracked like a whip against the rocky jaw of the big man. He staggered back against Forrie Cooke, roaring like a lion but Vic stepped in close before Budd could get up his big fists. He slammed a left to the guts, just above the gunbelt buckle, then threw a right cross that was a beauty of perfection and timing. Budd fell backward over a chair and Vic stepped across him just as Forrie Cooke dropped his hand for a draw. Vic knocked Forrie's gun hand to one side. His own Colt was jammed into Cooke's lean belly and Vic swung the man around between him and that cold-eyed bastard who had been watching the poker game. The man was on his feet but he did not move. His lower jaw had dropped when he had seen Chuck Budd hit the floor. No one around Banister had ever seen that done before.

Kile moved a little.

"Sit still, Mister Kile!" said Vic. "Put those manicured hands flat on the table!"

Kile did as he was told. There was a flush on his face and pure hell in his little eyes.

"By God, Standish!" said Forrie Cooke, "I'll kill you for this!"

Vic smiled coldly. "Not right now, Mister Cooke."

Chuck Budd got slowly to his feet. He wiped away a trickle of blood from the side of his mouth. "Put up that cutter, Standish," he said thinly, "and you and me will give the crowd a show, no holds barred."

"Like you gave Nick Earnshaw, eh, Budd?"

"It was an accident!"

"So you tell me."

Ben Cullen pushed his way through the quiet crowd. "All right, gentlemen," he said. "That's enough! Put up that gun, Vic. By godfrey, I had a feeling you'd get into some kind of trouble tonight."

Vic stepped back from Cooke, watching

the man's glacial blue eyes, waiting for the instant flicking that would alert Vic to Cooke's lightning draw, but it was not there. Vic sheathed his gun and walked to the bar. There was a bottle of rye there and a glass. He filled the glass and downed it, wiped his mouth, then walked along the length of the long bar, past the set faces of the watching men, to push his way through the batwings out on to the board sidewalk. He stepped off the walk and slanted across Main Street to where he had left his dun. He had had a bellyful of Banister that night, but he had come into Banister for two reasons that night, and the second one was to see Peg Earnshaw, and not on Jason Kile's account.

He untethered the dun and walked towards the side street that led to Mrs. Chapman's boarding house. He was still riled.He had been a damned fool to antagonize Jason Kile, but that was the way Vic Standish was built.

Vic turned into Third Street. The dun had begun to limp. Vic picked up his left rear hoof and felt a stone wedged into the frog. He felt for his pocketknife and as he did so, the feeling came over him that he was being watched. He opened the knife and quickly pried the stone from the frog. He dropped the hoof and turned. Even as he did so he saw the quick furtive movement in the shrubbery beside a darkened house. He dropped belly flat, clawing for his Colt just as twin flames flashed from the shrubbery and the roaring of a shotgun slammed back and forth between the buildings. The dun whinnied, then seemed to scream like a frightened woman. The dun fell heavily just as Vic fired from the ground. A man yelled in pain and then boots struck wood at the rear of the house.

The dun fell part way across Vic's right leg, pinning him to the soft ground. Vic cocked his six-gun and peered through the darkness. There was no sight nor sound of anyone now.

A man rounded the corner. "What the hell!" he said. It was Ben Cullen. He ran towards Vic and then stopped short as he saw the cocked six-gun. "Vic," he said. "It's me! Ben Cullen!"

Vic's face twisted. "Yeh," he said softly. "You sure got here in one helluva hurry, Ben."

The marshal stopped and stared at Vic. "What do you mean?"

"Somebody just tried to kill me, Ben. The easy way. A double-barrelled shotgun. Killed my dun."

Three more men rounded the corner. Vic

let down the hammer of his Colt. "Get the horse off my right leg," he said through set teeth.

They pried the horse back with boards and Vic pulled his leg free. He felt it. It wasn't seriously hurt. The soft ground, soaked by the heavy rains, had allowed the weight of the horse to push the leg into the earth. Ben pulled Vic to his feet. "Who was it, Vic?" he asked.

Vic wiped the cold sweat from his face. "I never saw him," he said. "But I think I might have winged him. I heard him yell."

Ben helped Vic to the porch of the house, then ran around to the back of it. Vic could hear him moving about in the shrubbery. Something clattered against wood. Something metallic. Then Ben appeared. "Nothing," he said. "I'll help you get to Doc Parch, Vic."

"Gracias."

Two other men gave Ben a hand to the doctor's office, Ben quickly left. The doctor examined the leg. "Nothing but a bruise, Vic," he said. He shoved his glasses up to his forehead. "By George," he said with a wry smile, "it didn't take you long to get into trouble, Vic. No, sir."

Vic stood up. His leg pained him but it

78

wasn't weak. He put on his hat and limped to the door.

"You ought to stay off that leg, Vic," said the doctor.

Vic turned and the blow from his eyes startled the doctor. "I haven't got time to stay off this leg," he said. He turned and left the office. Somewhere in Banister was the man who had tried to kill Vic Standish and Vic was almost sure he had winged him.

Vic limped back to the place where his dun still lay in the street. Curious people watched him as he freed his saddle and gear and slung it over his shoulder. He cut through the yard of the house where the ambusher had lain in wait for him. The moon was just showing its light down upon the town. Vic stopped beside a rain barrel. He thrust his free hand into it and felt cold metal. He pulled out a sawed-off double-barrelled shotgun. He held it up to the faint light. "Property of Marshal's Office, Banister, Nevada," he said aloud.

Vic dropped the deadly weapon back into its hiding place. Ben Cullen had moved almighty fast when he had gone to look for the would be killer, or a clue to his identity. It had given him just enough time to hide the shotgun in the barrel.

Vic walked up Third Street towards the

Chapman house. Amy Chapman was standing on the porch with a shawl about her thin shoulders. "There's no use you coming in here, Victor Standish," she harped. "Peggy isn't here."

"Where is she, ma'am?"

Amy arched her brows. "Didn't you know? She left here bag and baggage and moved out to the Lazy E. I argued with her. Peggy, I said..." Amy's voice trailed off. The tall lean man had gone. She could hear his boots thudding against the soft earth down the street. "Humph!" she said. "Well maybe this time whoever is trying to kill him won't miss!"

Chapter Six

The moonlight was silvery bright in the Valley of the Skull as Vic Standish emerged from the creek pass and looked up the long slopes towards the Lazy E buildings. He could see three rectangles of yellow light pinpointed against the dark mantle of trees behind the buildings. He spurred on the lathered sorrel he had bought in Banister and headed across a field towards the lights. He turned in the saddle and looked back into the pass. He had seen or heard nothing that would indicate that anyone was in there. Anyone alive, that is, for the night wind had seemed to be trying to speak to him in the voices of the restless spirits of the murdered. A warning he could not interpret.

He swung down from the sorrel when he reached the fence and tethered the tired animal to the gatepost. He carried his Winchester in his hands as he limped up the rise towards the lighted building. He recognized it now as the old, original ranch house of the Lazy E. Mark Earnshaw had built it when his family was small, building the larger structure in later years.

Vic wisely stopped behind a shed. Peg Earnshaw had learned to shoot along with her younger brothers and some said she was a match for any of them with the long gun with the possible exception of Buck. "Hello, the house!" he called out.

Nothing moved. A cold feeling came over Vic. He wet his dry lips. "Peg!" he called. "It's me! Vic Standish!"

Nothing. Not a sound or a movement. Nothing but the soughing night wind rustling the trees and brush.

Vic padded to the other side of the shed, then darted clumsily to the base of the windmill. "Peg!" he called out once more.

"Is that you Vic?" she answered.

He almost jumped. She had spoken from behind him. He turned slowly. She was standing beside the barn with a rifle in her slim hands. "Thank God," she said.

Vic nodded in satisfaction. She had learned her lessons well in the hard school of a feuding family. In a country where the hidden marksman could kill and the victim would never see him, indeed they might just hear the report of the gun as they died.

"I heard you ride up the slope," she said.

"Are you alone?"

She nodded. "Joe said he would bring out some men in the morning if I insisted on staying. He was going to come out with me tonight, but in his condition I thought I had better come alone."

"This is madness!"

She smiled. "Maybe, but you're here now, aren't you, Vic?"

"You didn't know I was coming."

"I stopped by to see Jim Fancher before I came here. He said he'd send you over when you got back."

"I haven't been back there."

"Then how did you find out?"

"Mrs. Chapman was *kind* enough to tell me." He laughed shortly.

"She was very upset about it, Vic. She means well. She wanted Dick to come out with me but she couldn't find him. I wasn't sorry."

"So?"

She made a face. "Dick still thinks he has property rights on me, Vic. His hands have a bad habit of straying. Come on into the house and have some coffee. You look awfully tired."

He limped beside her. She eyed him. "What's the matter with your leg, Vic?"

He opened the door for her and closed it behind him. He eyed the somewhat dusty interior of the old house. The faded curtains still hung drably over the windows. He drew them together, then hung sacking behind them to shield the interior of the room from outside view. As he did so he told Peggy of what had happened in Banister that night.

She paled and placed a slim hand at her lovely throat. "Who could it have been, Vic?"

He shrugged. "Any one of a number of men who have no reason to love me, Peg." He had not told her of finding Ben Cullen's shotgun in the barrel where Ben himself had cached it, probably figuring to come back for it later when the coast was clear. He had cursed himself a few times on the long ride out to the Lazy E for telling Ben of his finding of the Sharps cartridge case and slug in the creek pass. "I antagonized Jason Kile, Forrie Cooke and Chuck Budd earlier this evening. I wouldn't put it past any of the three of them."

"They must have moved fast to have been able to get into position in time to intercept you, Vic."

He looked away from her and warmed his hands at the open fireplace. "Yes."

She poured coffee for them and sat down. "You don't really think it was any of the three of them though, Vic."

He turned. "Why do you say that?"

She shrugged. "I just feel it," she said.

He sat down and rolled a cigarette. "I wish it was daylight," he said. He lighted the cigarette.

"Why, Vic?"

"I'd bundle you up and get you out of here."

"I'm not leaving, Vic."

"Maybe you haven't yet realized what you are up against? These men *kill* for what they want, Peg. They slaughtered enough of your family already," he said brutally.

"Maybe that is why I won't leave."

He threw up his hands in despair and anger. "You won't get men to work for you.

They'll shun this ranch as though it had the plague. No man wants to punch cattle knowing that at any minute someone is going to slide a 700 grain Sharps slug into his hide. You'll be hurrahed. Your cattle will be run off. Your waterholes will be poisoned. Your fences will be cut. You'll never know who is doing it, Peg. You can't keep this place going if they really mean to run you out. You can't hold this land, Peg!"

She stood up and walked to the fireplace, looking down into the dancing flames. "I can't just sell out and run away, Vic. I just can't!"

Vic walked towards her and as he did so he passed between the big lamp and one of the windows. Something smashed through the glass and an instant later, as he drove the girl into a corner with a shoulder, he heard the flat, booming roar of a big bore gun echo across the moon-lighted valley.

The gun spoke again and the slug shattered another window and drove into the log wall on the far side of the room. Vic forced the girl to the floor and bellied over towards the big Rochester lamp that sat on the table. As he reached up to put it out the rifle roared again and the slug slammed into the lamp knocking it across the room, scattering oil in all directions. A runnel of flame licked across the soaked table top and scurried in hot haste down a leg to nibble speculatively at the wide floor puncheons.

Vic snatched up a rug and beat out the flames. He flattened himself by sheer instinct hard against a wall a fraction of a second before a big slug whispered evilly of death as it passed through the very spot where he had been standing. He slid down to the floor and bellied over to Peg. "See what I mean?" he said fiercely. "Maybe they don't want to kill you. Maybe they do. In any case, this looks like a first class hurrahing, Peg!"

She smiled just a little. "I've been through a few of these before, Vic. When I was a little girl during the Skull Valley War, I was in this very house when the Dexter Boys shot it up."

Vic nodded grimly. "Yeah, and your father and his brother Bennett killed two Dexters and crippled one for life that very night by stalking them in the dark. So happens, Miss Earnshaw, we don't happen to have those two first-class fighting men with us here tonight."

Peg Earnshaw did an impulsive thing. She drew him close beside her on the dirty floor. "I have you, Vic," she whispered. She drew him closer and then kissed him. He drew back and stared at her. She kissed him again.

The kiss was punctuated by a shot that struck some canned goods on a shelf over their heads. Some of the cans rattled down and juice from one of them trickled down on them. Vic rolled away from the girl and crawled to get his rifle.

He stood up in a corner and peered quickly from a side window just as he saw the flash of a gun high on the slopes on the far side of the rushing creek. He slammed two shots towards the gun flame and then jumped back into shelter just as a slug sang thinly through the window from which he had fired. Gunsmoke rifted in the draughty room. "I thought you were nervous about being alone in this house with a man," he said over his shoulder.

There was a moment's hesitation and then she spoke from the darkness. "I was referring to Dick Chapman, Vic."

He grinned, despite the danger of their situation.

She picked up her rifle and crawled to where he was. "What do you think?" she said.

He rested his back against the wall. The hidden rifleman fired again. The slug shattered a frying pan that hung over the rust scaled kitchen range. "If you can keep him busy shooting from here, Peg, I might be able to stalk him. Not right now though. The way he, or *they* can shoot, no one could cross that creek bridge in the moonlight without getting a slug in his head."

Minutes ticked past. Then a gun spoke from further along the valley, a gun of lighter calibre. The slug whined from the cast iron stove. Shards of lead flew throughout the room. Peg winced in pain and placed a hand against her left cheek.

A cold hate was forming in Vic Standish. A cold and dangerous hate. The hurrahing was bad enough, but when Peg was hurt it hurt Vic, and it was going to hurt someone else a great deal more.

Vic crawled across the room and pushed open a bedroom door. He eyed the room. He could slip out of a window, work his way behind a shed and the barn, then round the corral in comparative safety, *if* the hidden marksmen were kept busy. He crawled back to Peg. "Listen," he said quietly. "I'm going to take a chance, moonlight or no, and try to get to where I can get a shot at them. It's up to you to keep them busy while I'm stalking them. But for God's sake don't take any chances. You'll be all right. I don't think they mean to rush the place. If they do..." He stopped talking and grinned like a hunting wolf. "I can spot them and get a few shots into them. Enough to teach them a lesson."

She kissed him. "Go on then, Vic, but don't take any chances. If it is too rough out there, come back, the two of us can hold this place against an army!"

It was Vic's turn to kiss her after those brave words and when he was done, there was a new wonder in the great grey eyes of Peg Earnshaw.

He crawled into the bedroom, walked quickly across it to a window and dropped lightly to the ground outside. He stepped behind the shed, reached the far end, dropped flat and crawled behind a watering trough to the barn, then followed the side of the barn until he reached the rear of it, where it pressed back into the thick woods. He hurried to the far end of the barn and inched along, flat to the ground behind the corral until he could worm his way through the damp tall grass to the rear of the cemetery. All the time he was moving he could hear the intermittent shooting from across the creek, with now and then a shot coming from the besieged house.

He worked his way beneath the wire fence of the graveyard and between the mounded graves and greystone tombstones until he could see the moonlighted panorama of the valley spread out before him. The creek rushed along, illuminated by the moon into a stream of sparkling quicksilver. The trees had etched shadows on the silvery patina of the ground. Only the eastern escarpment was dark in shadows, with hidden death in the form of skilled marksmen haunting the shadows.

There was a long pause in which the Valley of the Skull seemed as quiet and peaceful as in the old days when it had been a favourite camping ground of the Piutes. Even the brooding skull seemed almost benevolent as it looked down upon the valley.

Vic scanned the opposite slopes. In moving he had lost his bearings on where he had seen the gun flashes. He inched through the damp grass until he was right at the edge of the cemetery, pulled off his hat and placed his head between two clumps of grass. Time crawled on. There was no sound from the bullet pocked house. Vic hoped to God that one of those soft slugs hadn't ripped the life from Peggy Earnshaw. If it had, there would be a bloodbath in the Valley of the Skull to end all bloodbaths.

It was too quiet to suit Vic. He crawled along the fence line, then slipped beneath the wire fence to crawl into the grove of trees beyond the cemetery. The valley road was clearly lighted by the moon.

A shot ripped the quiet. It came from high on the escarpment several hundred yards south of the skull formation. It was answered immediately by a gun report from the house. Vic smiled in relief.

He worked his way through the rustling trees until he could see the side of the road no more than fifty feet away. He was north of where the last shot of the hidden rifleman had come from. Vic crawled through the thick grass and scattered brush until he made the roadside ditch. He was almost within fifty yards of the creek. The moon was on the wane, slanting its light down into the valley from the west. In a matter of an hour the valley would be dark until the false dawn. He couldn't wait that long to cross the bridge.

He knew now he was north of the place where the last shot had come from, and that the rifleman would be watching the house. There was a place where the road dipped into a hollow. He crawled to it, then swiftly rolled over and over, across the ruts until he landed in the ditch on the other side of the road. He crawled along the ditch for a hundred yards, then worked his way towards the creek through a scattered motte of willows.

It was quiet again. He'd have to wade or

swim the creek. Usually it was no more than two or three feet deep but the recent rains had raised it considerably. He made the bank of the creek. A gun rattled from high on the escarpment but he did not see the flash. Two shots sped from the darkened house.

Vic entrusted himself to the rushing water. It came up to his chest. Rifle held high he forced his way across despite the pain in his bruised leg until he could crawl out on the far bank, sluicing water from his clothing. He pulled off his boots and emptied them, then padded into the woods. He was half-way to the escarpment before he realized he was almost below the huge grinning face of the skull, lighted by the dying moon in such a way that although the naked rock of the skull top and most of the face was as white as dry bone, the eye sockets were thick with shadows. It was an eerie feeling to know he was being watched by that horrible caricature made by nature.

He stood up beside a thick-boled tree and eyed the silent escarpment. Before him was a moonlighted clearing. The last shots had come from a position far to his right. He studied the almost sheer rock wall trying to spot a place where he could ascend. If he was seen or heard while ascending he'd never make the top.

There was a brooding quietness about the valley again.

Vic wet his dry lips, ready for the quick rush across the clearing, hoping his leg would not let him down. He took one step into the bright moonlight and something seemed to warn him. He turned with a sudden feeling of acute and eerie alarm to stare up at that naked, grinning skull of stone. Even as he did so the eyes lighted up with red-orange flame and a roaring cry seemed to come from the gaping, toothless mouth. Something struck the thick tree just beside Vic. Something else struck the side of his head. He screamed harshly in fear and pain, then went down on his knees as he heard the fainter reports of a rifle from across the creek. Blood ran down the side of his face. He fought to regain his senses, then passed out completely.

There was a salty warmth in his mouth. He opened his eyes to look up into darkness. The moon was gone. The cold wind rushed moaning through the valley. Vic spat the blood from his mouth and pulled himself to his feet beside the tree. His questing fingers felt a three inch gash alongside his skull just above his right ear. He felt the tree and traced another gouge through the thick and scaly bark. The slug had barked the tree and

93

driven a piece of bark, or a shard of lead alongside his thick head.

He looked up at the dark shape of the skull and shivered a little. Superstitious fear had almost controlled him when those damned eyes had lighted up with hellfire. He knew now the rifleman had somehow gotten inside that landmark and had plainly seen Vic stepping into the clearing. He could have hardly missed at that range.

"Peg!" he said. He whirled, snatched up his rifle, ran heedlessly down the slope, dashed over the bridge, crossed the road and hurried through the grove past the cemetery. Even as he did he saw the first faint pewter coloured traces of the false dawn in the eastern sky high above the escarpment.

The house was dark and quiet when he reached it. "Peg!" he cried desperately. He was past all caring now about being shot at.

"Vic?" she said faintly from within the doorway.

They met on the sagging porch. He drew her inside the bullet wrecked room and kissed her again and again while the salty tears ran down her face and mingled with the sweetness of her soft lips.

Chapter Seven

Vic Standish led his sorrel up the last part of the escarpment trail, to the north of the skull formation, just as the sun topped the mountains to the east and shone down upon the back of the huge rock formation. Peggy led her bay mare up beside Vic's sorrel. "I haven't been up here for years," she said.

"The view is wonderful," said Vic drily. His skull still throbbed from the barking he had received and his leg still ached. He eased his hat back from the bandage that bound his head wound.

In the light of the dawn the valley had appeared deserted of anyone else but the two of them. There was no use in sitting in the bullet pocked house waiting for something to happen. They had ridden back through the woods, far north up the winding valley to make sure they were out of sight of anyone who might be watching them, then had crossed the creek at a ford, to ride up the long, transverse trail that reached the top of the escarpment, where it branched, the left hand trail continuing on down into a valley beyond the high rock wall that hemmed in Skull Valley. Beyond that valley the trail joined the Banister Road.

The terrain was quiet and peaceful under the morning sun. Sudden death seemed far away, but Vic Standish took no chances. They picketed the horses in a deep draw and continued south along the top of the rock wall towards the skull formation.

Vic had never really realized quite how large the skull formation was. It was a huge mass of rock, and the striations atop the skull seemed almost like the lines where the pieces of a human skull fitted neatly together. The ground was rough and treacherous, a jungle of shattered detritus and shintangle brush interlaced with catclaw and wait-a-bit-bush, that clung to clothing and flesh like barbed fish-hooks. To get to the side of the skull they had to literally plough their way through. The trail was a sort of labyrinth, winding and twisting back and forth, at times almost crossing itself.

Vic paused for breath at the rear of the formation. "I've never heard of this thing being hollow," he said.

"Nor I. Are you sure the shot was fired from *within* it, Vic?"

He nodded. "There's no way anyone could possibly have been around the eye sockets, or below it. I know the shot came from within the skull. It was quite a jolt to me, Peg." He grinned as he touched his aching head. "In more ways than one."

She shivered. "I can imagine." She shoved back her hat and wiped the beads of perspiration from her forehead. "What do you expect to find up here?"

He shrugged. "I don't know." He took out the makings and rolled a pair of cigarettes, thrusting one between her lips.

"I'm a lady," she protested.

He grinned again. He lighted her cigarette. "Happens I know you used to swipe the boys' smoking tobacco and sneak off behind the barn to have a drag or two, Peg."

She looked away. Vic placed a hand on her shoulder. He drew her close. Him and his big mouth. Her three big brothers were all gone now.

They went on after they had had their smoke. As the sun rose higher they rounded the skull but could find no way to enter it. Further along the escarpment they found empty cartridge cases, both of the Sharps Big Fifty and the more common .44/40. "There were at least two of them then," said Vic. He hefted the Sharps cartridge cases. "These are fired from a devilishly long and heavy rifle," he continued. "I can't imagine a local waddie carrying one of them around hanging to his saddle. It just doesn't make sense to me."

She nodded. "Whoever uses it might keep it cached somewhere until he needs it to hurrah anyone with it."

"Or to kill," he said. He looked back at the skull. "That was a close one last night."

"Thank God he missed that time," she said.

"I wonder?" he mused. "If it *is* the same marksman, he could have hardly missed me, Peg. I was standing down there as big as life. Forgive me for saying so, but he killed your father and brother from a far greater range, in shifting light. He placed a bullet accurately into the lantern that was beside your cousin Joe. Joe insisted that it was a warning. I didn't quite believe him then. I do now."

She looked up at him. "But why would he have deliberately missed *you?* They'd want you out of the way, Vic. They tried to kill you in Banister. Did they try to miss then?"

He shook his head. "Hardly. I have had more than a few close ones in my time, Peg. That was about as close as any of them. That shotgun would have torn off my head. I still don't know what warned me. A second's hesitation and I would have been killed."

They back-trailed to the skull formation and scouted all around it. If there was any way to get into that rock formation other than dangling a rope from atop it, then sliding down it to swing into one of the gigantic eye sockets, it was so well concealed that neither one of them could find it. "Beats me," said Vic. He pulled a thorn from his boot sole and looked at Peg. "What do you aim to do now?"

She leaned back against a rock and let her hat fall back from her lovely titian hair. Her checkered shirt was partway open and he could see the faintest suggestion of the cleft between her full breasts as she looked out into the great valley below them. His heart was full with the love of this young woman. Fool that he had been to think that he could forget her. A coldness swept over him when he thought of how she might just have married Dick Chapman.

Peggy looked up at him, then narrowed her eyes, for she seemed to read his thoughts. "Do you still want me to sell out, Vic?"

"I don't really know, Peg."

"Would you, Vic?"

He did not answer. He felt for the makings.

"Vic?"

He looked at her. "By God, Peggy," he said harshly, "they'd have to kill me to keep me from fighting for my rights."

"There's your answer," she said simply.

"Me and my big mouth again!"

She looked beyond him. "Riders," she said.

He turned quickly, instinctively reaching for his rifle. Five horsemen had debouched from the pass and were riding up towards the ranch buildings.

"Can't see who they are from here," said Vic.

"I don't think our enemies would ride right up to the ranch in broad daylight," she said.

They walked back to their horses and led them down the trail, then crossed the creek and entered the woods on the far side. When they reached the vicinity of the ranch, Vic went ahead. He saw Joe Dunlap seated on the front porch of the old house. Jim Fancher was leaning against a post whittling. Dick Chapman was examining some of the bullet holes in the house. Two other men were near the fence that ran behind the house, playing cards atop a barrel.

Vic waved Peggy on and the two of them rode up to the house. "Thank God," said Joe Dunlap. His face was flushed from his drinking and his hands were a little unsteady.

Jim Fancher shook his head as he saw

100

them. "What happened here, Vic? We got right scared when we got here and saw the mess. Are you all right, boy? Were you hit bad?"

"Just a creasing," said Vic. "Peg is all right."

"I argued with her about coming out here," said the rancher.

"So did I," said Joe. "She's more Earnshaw than Dunlap. You can't ever argue with an Earnshaw once they set their bull heads."

"You might learn something from the Earnshaws," said Peg coldly.

Dick Chapman walked past Vic as though he didn't exist and took Peg by the arm. "You're coming back to Banister with me," he said.

She pulled away. "Oh, stop it, Dick!"

"All alone out here."

"Vic was with me."

"He was? Alone out here? People will start talking, Peg!"

She tilted her head to one side. "Who, Dick?" she asked sweetly. "Your aunt?"

He flushed. "Well, not exactly. It's being out here with a man like Vic Standish."

"That's enough, Dick," said Jim angrily.

Dick turned. "Keep out of this, Jim."

Vic leaned against a porch post. He was

101

dead weary of the quibbling. "Shut up, Chapman," he said quietly. "You always did have a big mouth."

The tall man turned and as he did so Vic could see the holstered Colt beneath the man's coat. "The last time you and I tangled, Standish," he said thinly, "you had the edge."

Vic straightened up. "What are you driving at?"

"You said the next time I drew a gun on you, you'd kill me."

Jim Fancher walked quickly in between them. "It wasn't my idea that he come along, Vic," he said. He turned. "Now, Dick, you keep quiet. We can't make sense with Peggy if you two gamecocks are clattering your spurs. I want no more of it!"

"Blessed are the peacemakers," said Chapman with a sneer. He turned on a heel and walked away.

Joe Dunlap looked up at Peggy. "I brought two hands," he said. "Offered them double wages to work until we got organized out here. It was the only way I could get 'em, Peg."

"Two men aren't a tenth of what you'll need," said Jim.

"I'll stay," said Vic.

Jim waved a hand. "And get killed! You're

a marked man, Vic. After tangling with Kile, Cooke and Budd in Banister last night and nearly getting drygulched in the street, not to mention what happened out here, how long do you think it will be unti they get you too?"

"I wasn't thinking of retiring," said Vic.

Jim walked to Peg and took her hands in his. "Listen, Peg," he said earnestly. "Do you want Vic to get killed and maybe Joe too? Maybe you'll get ambushed as well. It just doesn't make sense. The ranch isn't worth it."

"It is to me, Jim."

He shook his head. "Come stay with me and Vic," he said. "Sell this place. Forget about it."

"I can't do that, Jim."

The rancher shrugged in despair. "I don't know what to say. I've a good mind to ride to the county seat and get some action here. They know me there. They know Jim Fancher. Everyone in this part of Nevada knows me. If necessary I'll go to the governor to get action. This bloodshed and shooting belongs elsewhere, not in this country!"

"Meanwhile we fight," said Vic.

"I didn't ask you to come back to get killed, boy," said the rancher.

"I'm here, Jim," said Vic simply.

Joe stood up. "I'll get the two men, Peg. It's all I could get. They were working for Jim, but Jim said he could get along without them."

"Good men," said Jim. "Hey, boys!"

The two men came towards the house. One of them was a short, bench-legged man of middle age with a gap toothed smile, and the other was a dark looking, taciturn man of some kind of mixed blood.

"The short one is Ace Miles, the tall man is Carl Rivera, Peggy," said Jim.

"Do you men know what you're getting into here?" asked Peg quietly.

Miles nodded. "Always glad to help a lady," he said. "Anyways I always liked your Paw and brothers, ma'am."

Rivera looked about. "I will stay as long as you need me, Miss Earnshaw."

"It might be dangerous."

River shrugged. "All life is dangerous, is it not?"

Joe Dunlap rubbed his bristly jaws. "Guess we better check the range," he said. "There's all the saddle horses out there somewheres too. We'd better try to round them up." He led the two hands with him to their horses. They mounted and rode off through the woods.

Dick came towards Peggy. "I saw Jason Kile this morning, Peggy. He said his offer is still good."

"The place is not for sale."

"I told him that."

Jim Fancher took off his hat and slapped his leg with it. "Well, I'd best be getting back." He looked at Vic. "You aim to stay here?"

"I think I had better, Jim."

"It's fine with me, Vic. I guess I would do the same if I was your age. I'm going to ride into town and send a wire to the county seat. Don't take any chances. It's possible they might have that mess cleaned up about the sheriff. If not, I aim to take steps myself to settle this bloodshed."

"Just how?" asked Dick Chapman sarcastically.

"Vigilantes," said Jim. There was a spark of the old fire in his eyes. "We had them here right after the war. We can organize again. I'm not so old I can't ride and fight once more for law and order!"

"Hear, hear!" said Dick.

Jim turned on a heel and walked to his horse.

"He's scared half to death," said Dick.

"He's still twice the man you are," said Peggy.

Dick flushed. He looked at her. "For the last time, are you coming with me?"

"No, Dick, and you have no right to bother me about it."

"I did once, you know."

"That time is past."

Dick looked at Vic. "If it hadn't been for you, Peg would have been my wife."

"You had a whole year to work it, Dick," said Vic quietly. "What's the matter? Losing the famous Dick Chapman charm?"

For a fraction of a second Vic thought the man was going to draw, but instead Chapman turned on a heel and walked to his fine black mare and mounted it. He rode towards the pass road, dashing past Jim Fancher as he rode towards the pass too.

"His ego has been badly hurt," said Peggy.

"I'd like to hurt more than his ego, Peg."

She walked to the house. "I'm a little afraid of him, Vic, not for my sake, but for yours. He'll never forgive you for what you did to him the day of the funeral."

"I'm worried."

"You should be. Dick can be dangerous, Vic. Don't ever underestimate him."

Vic grinned. "I'm more afraid of his aunt than I am of him."

She smiled. "I see your point."

He followed her into the house. "You'll need supplies," he said. "I can borrow them from Jim if you like. He's still stocked from the days when he ran a big spread. It will save us a trip into Banister. I can get a team and a spring wagon there and load it, and be back here before dark, Peg. Will you be all right by yourself?"

"I'll have to get used to being alone, Vic."

He kissed her, then left the house. He mounted the sorrel and rode towards the pass. The sun was filling it with pure light as he entered it. There was no sign of life. The place was as peaceful as a church. Still, as he rode along the road, with his rifle across his thighs and his eyes flicking from height to height, watching for any movement or reflection of sunlight on metal he had the feeling that he was being watched.

He reached the end of the pass without incident and rode towards the F Bar M. He was crossing Piney Creek ford when the sun flashed brilliantly from something on the heights. Something like polished glass. Almost as though someone with a pair of powerful fieldglasses was watching Vic Standish as he rode towards the buildings.

It took longer than Vic had anticipated to get the supplies together. He loaded the wagon, then hunted cartridges for his rifle and pistol. When he came out of the house it was to see the valley filling with dusk light. His stomach was in a knot from lack of food. By this time Joe Dunlap and the two hands should be back at the Lazy E headquarters, so Peg would be safe enough. Vic hated the thought of driving that wagon through the dark pass but he had no choice. Meanwhile he might as well grub up.

He cooked a simple meal and made a pot of coffee. He ate quickly, then leaned back in his chair to roll a cigarette. As he lighted it he noticed the time on the faded face of the waggle-tail clock. It was after six o'clock. He jumped to his feet and reached for his rifle and hat and as he did so he heard the booming roar of a heavy calibre gun and he hit the floor through long practice in such matters. The slug whipped through an open window and buried itself in the guts of the clock. Springs and gears flew out of the shattered case and scattered on the floor. Vic doused the light and crawled out onto the back porch. He lay there flat behind a big log that Little Mac had carved into a bench seat. Not even a Sharps slug could penetrate through that.

There was no sign of life. The wind shifted and the windmill ground into slow life. A horse whinnied from the corral. The creek murmured softly in its course to the south-east. Vic lay there for twenty minutes, not wanting to stay and not wanting to leave, but he couldn't be bluffed forever. He had to get back to Peg.

He took his courage into his hands and walked to the wagon. He mounted the seat and placed his rifle close beside him. The moon was not up yet. He'd rather drive in darkness than to have that clear silvery light revealing his every move. "Growl you can," he said drily, "but go you must." He slapped the reins on to the backs of the team and drove for the ford with his sorrel trotting along behind the wagon.

Thank God that Jim Fancher had not been in the house. The warnings he had received had almost unnerved the old man. His heart must have failed had he heard that slug whip through the window out of the darkness to shatter the old clock. It had startled Vic Standish badly enough.

He entered the pass with his heart in his mouth and drove steadily through it, with the sound of the wheels and hoofs echoing back from the sheer walls, loud enough to alert anyone who might be listening. But they couldn't see to shoot unless they came right down to the roadside, and Vic Standish was ready with a fully loaded Winchester.

He reached the end of the pass just as the first faint rays of the moon showed down into Skull Valley to touch the rock formation that had given the place its name.

The house was lighted and a wraith of smoke hung low over the shake roof. The odour of cooking food came to Vic on the night wind.

As he reached the Texas gate he heard a man call out. "Who is it?" Vic recognized the voice of Carl Rivera. He called back and then opened the gate. He drove the wagon into the barn. Rivera came in behind him. Vic turned. "Everything all right, Carl?"

"Yes and no, Vic."

"What do you mean?"

"We found the horses that had been driven off."

"And?"

"All eight of them had been shot to death over near Willow Crick."

"That figures."

Carl nodded. "That's what Joe said. I guess there ain't any doubt about who did it."

"No."

"You want us to stand guard tonight, Vic?"

"I'm not the boss, Carl." Vic got down

from the wagon and picked up his rifle. "Joe is."

"Yeh," said the tall man. "Only he ain't here."

"Where is he?"

Carl grinned. "Ran out 'a red-eye. He went back into Banister for more."

Vic shook his head. He walked towards the house. The thought came to him that maybe Jim Fancher and Dick Chapman were thoroughly right after all. It might be a hopeless fight ending in death for all of them if they stayed at the ranch.

His mind changed when he walked into the house and saw Peggy standing at the stove, dressed in gingham, with a neat little apron about her, and her hair done up. Her face was flushed and warm from the heat of the stove as he kissed her. A man must fight for his woman and for what he thinks is right. It's as simple as that.

Chapter Eight

The smell of smoke came to Vic Standish. He opened his eyes and clawed for his rifle. He rolled from the floor pallet and glanced up to see the eerie red light of a big fire showing through the shattered windows of the living-room. The crackling of burning wood came to him. He ran to the windows and saw flames licking steadily up the side of the barn, frying out the moisture from the rain soaked wood.

"What is it, Vic?" called Peg from the bedroom.

"Barn is ablaze!" yelled Vic. "Carl! Ace!"

Ace poked his head out from under the blanket that covered. He sniffed the air. "Fire? Where's Carl!"

Vic opened the rear door of the house and ran out onto the sagging porch. He could see the entire side of the barn now and could hear the frantic screaming of the horses corralled beyond it. He sprinted awkwardly for the corral. The whole area was illuminated by the roaring flames. The interior of the barn was an inferno. Great flakes of burning wood soared upward in the fierce draught of heat. They floated towards the creek like blazing butterflies.

Vic tore at the railings of the corral while the horses dashed about the muddy interior in a perfect frenzy of fear. He glanced over his shoulder to see Carl Rivera running through the smoke towards him.

"Drive them this way, Carl!" yelled Vic.

The tall man ran to the gate of the corral and tore off his hat to wave it at the frenzied horses. Somewhere across the valley there was a spot of flame, as though one of the embers from the roaring fire had alighted in the dark woods. The faint sound of a gun report came drifting across the creek. Carl Rivera fell forward into the corral and lay still. Vic hit the damp ground just as the horses tore through the gap he had made in the fence. He saw Ace Miles running towards the corral. "Hit the dirt, Ace!" screamed Vic. The little man slid to a halt and dropped to the ground. The gun flashed again and the slug rapped into a corral post.

Vic bellied through the muck of the corral until he reached Carl. He rolled the man over. He saw death beginning to film the man's eyes. "God damn him to everlasting hell," mouthed the dying man. He went limp in Vic's arms. Blood gushed in a red spate from his mouth and the firelight glistened from the bright fluid of life.

Vic lay flat, peering beneath the lower rail of the corral. No man could cross that firelit ground and be safe from a bullet. Vic looked towards Ace. The little man had vanished.

The barn was engulfed in flames and embers were dropping on the other buildings

113

of the spread. A shed was blazing. A spot of flame was widening on the roof of the house. Peggy darted from the rear of the house and vanished behind an out-building, carrying two Winchesters. Trust Peg to think about bringing out the rifles.

Vic wet his lips. He peered through the smoke towards the creek. The sky was dark and overcast with no sign of the moon. Even as he watched he felt the first great drops of rain strike his back. A shift came in the wind and it turned cold, lashing the flames into a perfect fury of destruction, and then as the roof of the house caught fire, the rain began to fall heavily in a perfect deluge. For fifteen minutes the elements fought against each other, until at last the silvery downpour won. In forty-five minutes the fires were out, though the roof of the house was ruined, the shed was half eaten away and the barn was nothing but a blackened and gutted ruin.

Vic shivered. He was soaked to the skin. He took a chance that the veils of rain would conceal him and he walked crouched over to the rear of the corral and then into the dripping woods. "Peg?" he called out.

She arose from behind a log. She was shivering in the wet cold. "How is Carl?" she asked.

Vic did not answer. He looked away.

"Vic, is he...? Vic?" she almost screamed.

Vic nodded. He placed an arm about her shaking shoulders. "Now you can see how foolish it is to stay here and fight, Peg," he said.

There was no answer from her. Even the bravest have moments of grave doubt when the courage of their convictions is not as firm as it has been.

"It wasn't his fight," she said.

Vic led her to one of the outbuildings. It was the old bunkhouse of the Lazy E. He started a fire in the pot-bellied stove. "Stay here," he said. He took one of the rifles and walked outside. The heaviest downpour had passed now that it had defeated the fire. A light drizzle misted across the dark valley. By the light of a few flickering embers Vic could see fairly well. If the killer was still across the creek he couldn't see through the rain and mist. Maybe he had done his job for the night and was satisfied, like a vampire who had fed on one of his victims and is sated until ready to walk again in search of more blood.

Vic walked behind the ruined barn. He stopped short. There was an empty oil can lying in the high grass. He picked it up and smelled coal oil. He turned it around. It was faintly marked with painted letters. "F Bar M," he said quietly. It was one of the full oil cans he had brought from Jim's ranch just the evening before. He rubbed his jaw. He had placed the stores in the kitchen of the old house. A cold feeling came over him as he realized that the arsonist had evidently taken the coal oil from the kitchen while Vic and Ace had been sleeping in the next room. Carl had been on guard. Why hadn't he seen the prowler? Why hadn't he given the alarm? It was no use in blaming the man now. He was beyond blame.

Vic walked to the corral and to where Carl lay in the rain. He leaned the rifle against the corral fence and bent to pick up the dead man. As he did so he caught the faint, but unmistakable odour of coal oil on the man's blood soaked shirt. Vic squatted on his heels and eyed the set white face of the dead man. Was it possible that Carl had set the fire? If so, for what purpose? He had been shot down by the unseen killer as so many others had been shot down before him. Vic stood up and looked across the top rail of the corral. He turned and looked towards the rear of the corral. An icy feeling came over him. Vic himself had been in a line with Carl when Carl had ran to the gate. Maybe the killer had been aiming at Vic instead of Carl.

In a split second the tall F Bar M man had stepped into the line of fire. Or was Vic thinking up something that really wasn't true? He picked up his rifle and walked to the rear of the corral. There was no sign of Ace Miles anywhere around the place. The little man had been frightened, Vic supposed. Still...

Peg was warming herself at the stove. She turned to look at Vic, and once again she displayed that uncanny sense of intuition of hers. "What's wrong, Vic? This is more than just a hurrahing again, isn't it?"

"It's another murder, if that's what you mean."

She narrowed her lovely eyes. "Why would they kill Carl?"

"I wonder."

She came close to him. "What are you holding back, Vic?" she asked.

He told her of the coal oil can and the odour of the fuel on Rivera's shirt, and of the fact that Carl had been in a dead line with Vic when the shot had been fired. "Did you hear anyone in the kitchen during the night, Peg?" he asked.

She shook her head. "It doesn't seem possible that Carl Rivera would have deliberately started a fire."

"The barn was pretty wet, Peg. The hay

and straw would have been damp. Even if it had been slow in starting it couldn't have gained the headway it had when I first saw it without alerting Carl while he was on guard. Unless he had wandered off or fallen asleep."

"Yes," she said thoughtfully.

The rain slashed down again, drumming on the roof of the bunkhouse. Water began to drip through holes in the old roof. Some of it hissed on the hot stove. Vic shook his head. "The thing that bothers me, is that with all this killing, no one, or at least we too, have never seen the killer. It gives me an eerie feeling, Peg."

She nodded. "But it is a man of flesh and blood doing the killing."

"He might be of flesh and blood," he said grimly, "but with the soul of a demon. He kills as though he was swatting flies."

"You said 'he', Vic. Why not 'they'?"

He felt for the makings and rolled two cigarettes before he answered. "The last words Carl said were: 'God damn him to everlasting hell', Peg."

She placed a cigarette between her lips and bent her head forward for a light. "Almost as though he knew who it was," she said.

"Unless he meant it in general."

118

She looked up at him. "But you don't think so?"

He shrugged. *"Quien sabe?"* He paced back and forth. He looked at her. "I have been wondering who tried to kill me that night in Banister. The only suspect I have so far is Ben Cullen."

"It's pretty well known around Banister that Ben is more than just friendly with Jason Kile. Dick Chapman told me that Ben and Jason have had their heads together a few times. Ben is quite a politician, Vic. You antagonized Jason Kile. Kile won't forget that. He and his boys had hardly time to get ahead of you into the street to try and kill you."

"Yes. And, come to think of it, Ben was in the Banister House Bar when I left! I had forgotten that!"

She shivered a little. "It's almost as though you were walking around in a world peopled by those who mean to kill you and you haven't any real idea who they are."

"It's easier to face danger when you know what it is," he agreed.

"What shall we do now, Vic?"

He picked up his rifle. "I'm going to find Ace," he said.

The rain had died away again. Mist was swirling up from the unseen creek bottoms.

There was an eerier appearance in the area of the Lazy E buildings, at least those that hadn't been burned to the ground. Here and there in the thick, wet beds of ashes an ember winked like a red eye watching Vic. The mingled odours of fresh rain, smoke and wet burned wood clung about the area like a pall.

Vic hunted high and low. There was no sign of the little man. He had vanished completely, probably scared half to death by sudden fire and more sudden death.

When the cold light of dawn penetrated through the drifting mists in the Valley of the Skull there was still no trace of Ace Miles. The only two humans in the silent valley were Peggy Earnshaw and Vic Standish. Vic had rounded up two of the horses, the others had vanished as Ace Miles had vanished.

"There's no object in staying here now," said Vic as he finished the meal Peg had cooked atop the bunkhouse stove.

"I can't leave, Vic," she said.

"Why stay? There's nothing left to defend. The land is still yours. They can't burn that from under you."

"What about the cattle?"

Vic drained his coffee cup. "Maybe we can drive them over to the F Bar M. If we can't get men to work on the Lazy E, we can at

120

least get men to work on the F Bar M. Jim won't mind having your cattle graze on his land."

She walked to the window and looked out across the misty valley. "I hate to leave," she said.

"We have no choice. Besides, I have an idea that whoever is behind all this wants the Lazy E badly enough to kill for it. They want you to sell the place and think these killings and hurrahings will force you to do so. But if you leave the land, and don't sell it, they'll have to show their hand if they want the land desperately."

She turned. "I never thought of it that way. I suppose I have been obstinate and foolhardy, Vic."

"No more than most women," he said with a grin.

There was a job he had to do before they left the Valley of the Skull. He had to bury Carl Rivera. He knew better than to bother having Carl brought into Banister. There was no law in the county. One dead cowpoke more or less didn't matter anymore. Before he let Peg come to the grave with him, he did something that turned his stomach a little, but it was a necessary evil as far as he was concerned. The bullet that had killed Carl had struck him close beside the upper spine,

121

lodging beside the man's heart. When he had taken it from the wound there was no doubt about what type of rifle it had been fired from. The Sharps Big Fifty had killed again.

They buried Carl, and Vic said a few words over the mounded grave. He still had his suspicions of Carl, but the man was dead. It was the living killer, or killers that Vic was interested in, not the harmless dead.

They left the valley by way of the winding, tortuous trail that cut through the hills to the west of the Valley of the Skull. Vic hadn't wanted Peg to be exposed to whoever had killed her father and brother in the creek pass. Beyond the hills, not far from Willow Creek they saw the swelling bodies of the dead horses that Joe Dunlap, Carl Rivera and Ace Miles had found the day before. Each of them had been killed by a bullet through the head. Once again Vic did a little probing, extracting three bullets from the heads of as many horses. They were all .44/40's. He eyed the swelling carcasses.

"What's wrong, Vic?" she said.

Vic shoved back his hat and felt for the makings. "Odd," he said quietly as he began to roll a smoke. "These horses were driven from your place some days ago."

"Yes?"

He looked up at her. "There are still wolves and coyotes in these hills. Plenty of them."

She shivered a little. "I've heard them many a time."

"Look at these carcasses. They haven't yet been touched by wolves or coyotes."

"So?"

"Another thing: From their condition, I'd say they hadn't been dead more than twenty-four hours."

"Are you sure, Vic?"

"I'd stake my life on it."

She accepted a cigarette from him and blew a reflective ring of smoke. "They couldn't have been dead very long when the boys found them then."

"The thought has struck me too, Peg."

He looked across the range, now lighted by a watery looking sun. Something was wrong, definitely wrong, yet he had no solid clues, no definite lead. "I wish I could find Ace Miles," he said. "Carl told me about these horses, but he didn't mention anything about the time they had been killed. That doesn't mean anything of course. Unless he was deliberately concealing something. Ace has vanished, but whether from fright or guilt we don't know."

"There's always my beloved cousin," she

said quietly. "Joe was here with Carl and Ace."

He nodded. He mounted his horse and they rode across the rugged Lazy E range. It was good ranching country, but not on a par with the F Bar M and other ranches further south in the more open country. The thought came again to Vic that there was something more about the Lazy E that was valuable. *Something* that was so valuable to *someone* that he, or they, if there were more than one person involved, were willing to kill, and kill again, to get the Lazy E. It was beyond Vic's understanding.

Close to the border line between the Lazy E and the rolling range of the F Bar M, they could see the cattle of the Lazy E dotting the grasslands. Vic looked at her. "How many head was your father running, Peg?"

She shrugged. "I don't know, Vic. As you know, I was teaching school in town. Dad thought it was best for me to stay in town as long as there was any sign of trouble. He seemed to have a premonition."

"Would Joe know?"

"Probably. He was helping Buck ramrod the ranch. Sometimes I think Dad kept Joe on out of sheer pity for him."

They forded the West Fork of Piney Creek and entered onto F Bar M land. Far across the open country they could see some of the few head that Jim Fancher still ran on his spread. "This is good range, Peg," said Vic. "Jim may decide to keep on ranching. Since Little Mac died, I guess he has lost considerable heart. I really didn't want to come back, but I couldn't turn Jim down. In a way I wish he would sell out and leave this country. He's a badly frightened man, Peg."

She nodded. "That's what Amy Chapman told me more than once."

"Why Amy?" he looked at her curiously.

She arched her eyebrows. "Didn't you know Jim had been sparking Amy for a time?"

He rolled his eyes upwards. "God forbid," he said.

She smiled. "Oh, she isn't that bad, Vic. She even considered becoming engaged to him some months ago, but she refused absolutely to marry him if she had to live out here. Amy Chapman is strictly city folks, Vic."

"Maybe that's why he has been thinking of selling out. Maybe I could make a deal with him, to run the ranch that is, and he could go into retirement. It seems a shame to let a ranch like the F Bar M sit here in the sun without cattle being raised on it."

He glanced sideways at her. "If I can make a deal with Jim, Peg, there is something you could do for me."

"Yes?"

"Sell the Lazy E, marry me, and come to the F Bar M to raise cattle and kids."

She flushed a little. "I'll consider it, Vic. But not until we run down the men who have killed so wantonly. I could never rest knowing they were still loose in the world, Vic. Never! Never, do you understand?"

"Amen," he said. He leaned towards her, drew her close and kissed her.

Chapter Nine

Jim Fancher was dead tired. There were new lines on his face and a new hopelessness in his voice. He stirred his coffee and looked up at Vic and Peggy. "There'll be no action from the sheriff. At a time when we need law and order as we never have before, the county officials and Sheriff Cranmer are still fighting it out. Politics has taken the place of justice in this county." He looked up at the shattered clock still hanging on the kitchen wall. "That shot was meant for *me*, Vic, not for you. Thank God he missed."

"It was close enough," said Vic. He sipped his coffee. "Then it's all right with you to drive the Lazy E cattle on to the F Bar M?"

Jim nodded. "You take over, Vic. You can manage the place." He smiled wearily. "It will be yours some day. It's in my will," he said with a fatalistic tone.

"You'll be around for a long time," said Peggy.

"I don't know," he said quietly. "I *used* to be a fighting man in the old days and during the war."

"You still are at heart," said the young woman.

Jim shook his head. "I'm getting too old for this sort of life."

Vic stood up and walked to the stove. He picked up the big coffee pot. "I don't like to say this, Jim, but there's more than one person around here who thinks you could have kept out of things by keeping your mouth shut."

"I talk when I see injustice!" snapped the rancher.

Vic refilled the coffee cups. "Most of the talking you seem to have done concerns the killings of Norm and Nick Earnshaw by Forrie Cooke and Chuck Budd. I talked to

Ken Brucker the other night and he seems to think Norm was killed fairly enough, if a killing can be considered fair."

"Bosh!" snapped Jim.

Vic knew better than to rile the old man, but he had to make sense to Jim whether he liked it or not. "There were witnesses, Jim. The coroner's verdict was that Cooke killed in selfdefence."

Jim's eyes narrowed. "You talk like a Kile man."

Vic ignored him. "Nick Earnshaw was holding his own with Chuck Budd when he was driven back against a spoke sticking out of the wall. You don't think Budd deliberately planned that, do you?"

"I was there I tell you! I saw the whole thing! They *planned* to get rid of Nick."

"Rather an odd way to do it," said Vic drily, "when they got rid of others simply by drygulching them, and no one the wiser. The coroner said Budd was fighting in selfdefence."

Jim rolled his eyes upwards. "My God," he said hoarsely.

Vic kept on. "Ken Brucker was there the night Nick was killed. He said it was the opinion of quite a few watching the fight that it wasn't rigged."

"Ken Brucker is a drunken fool!"

Vic sipped his coffee. "The thing that strikes me as being odd is the fact that Ben Culen wasn't around to stop either one of those fights."

Jim snorted. "He knew better."

"You think he's one of the combine you mentioned?"

"I'd swear on it!"

Vic nodded. "I'm beginning to agree. My advice to you, Jim, is to get out of this area for awhile. Go to the county seat and see if you can get some action. I'll run the ranch."

"Well, I'm scairt, I'll admit, but I don't like the idea of anyone running me off my ranch."

"No one is running you off your ranch," said Vic patiently. "I'll take care of it. You were warned a few times. Get away from here until things cool off and until we can find out who is behind these killings."

"With no law? Who's going to find out who killed all those fine men?"

"You mentioned vigilantes," said Vic.

Jim snorted again. "There isn't a man I'd trust myself to ride with around here except you, Vic. Who knows who is part of the combine and who isn't? I don't trust anyone and neither do you, and you know it."

"Then I'll appoint myself a one man vigilante committee, Jim," said Vic.

"You'll get a Sharps slug through the head. Mark my words!"

"Go pack," said Vic firmly.

When Jim had left the room they could hear him grumbling as he packed in his bedroom. Vic looked at Peg. "I'll feel better if he isn't around. We might be safe enough here, but if that slug was meant for Jim, and I think it was, he'll be better off scrapping at the county seat than sitting around here worrying himself sick."

"He may be right though," she said. She studied Vic. "Who can we trust?"

Vic did not answer her. He walked outside. The same problem had been bothering him.

She came out behind him. "You can't drive those cattle from my range to this range alone, Vic. I can help of course and we can get Joe to help, if he's sober enough. Jim has two more men out on this range. They could help."

Vic thudded a fist against a porch post. "A woman, a drunk, and two old crocks! Those two men you speak about are Henry Fish and Jake Truro. Henry is close to seventy years old, Peg. Jake Truro would run if you popped a champagne cork within half a mile of him."

She looked out across Piney Creek,

shimmering in the bright sunlight. "I can sell the cattle," she said quietly.

"You'd never get your price for them, Peg," said Vic. "The market is down as it is. Some sharpie would come in and offer you bottom prices. Your father built up that herd to what it is, Peg. It's one of the best in the county. You can't afford to sell them."

Jim stamped out onto the porche. "Hitch up my buckboard, Vic," he said. "I'll stay in Banister tonight and go on to the county seat tomorrow."

Vic glanced at him. "You could make it all the way to Bald Rock by dusk, Jim."

The older man flushed a little. "Well, I ain't told you this, Vic, but I been payin' court to Amy Chapman. I can't just go scootin' out of the town without seein' Amy, can I?"

Vic shrugged. "I guess not." He walked to the corral to get a team.

"She's a fine woman, Vic!" called out Jim, as though in selfdefence.

Vic did not answer. In addition to being the pinnacle of respectability in town, Amy Chapman had one other characteristic that Vic disliked. She was a pennypincher, penurious and greedy, and the almighty dollar was rated even higher in her small mind than the façade of respectability she had constructed about herself. If Amy Chapman ever married Jim Fancher she'd never live on the F Bar M, as Peg had said. She was city folks. Furthermore, if Jim had named Vic as his heir in his will, leaving the fine F Bar M to Vic, it certainly wouldn't remain that way once Amy Chapman sank her spurs into old Jim and slipped a curb bit in his mouth. She had no use for Vic in the first place. It would probably kill Jim to have to live in Banister, wearing a tie and collar every blessed day, attending church and social work meetings with Amy, the very essence of respectability.

"Respectability!" said Vic to himself as he led the team towards the buckboard. He looked up to see Jim standing by the buckboard.

"You mean Amy, don't you, Vic?" said Jim.

Vic nodded. "She sort of overplays the part, Jim."

"She's a fine woman," said Jim. He lighted a cigar. "Maybe you think I'll cut you out if I marry Amy?"

"It's your ranch, Jim. I didn't come back here for that reason."

The older man nodded. "I knew that. That's why I aim to leave you aplenty, Vic. I know you think Amy will hog-tie me and try to teach me manners, and run my life. Well, she won't make me forget *you*, Vic. You stand aces with ol' Jim here. Don't you ever forget it either!"

Vic smiled. "Thanks, Jim," he said. He harnessed the team and placed Jim's gear in the back of the vehicle. He gripped the older man's hand then waved as Jim drove the team towards the Piney Creek ford. He was glad to see him go. Maybe by the time Jim got back from the county seat things would be different. On the other hand, maybe Jim had called the shot when he had warned Vic that he might get a Sharps slug through the head.

He walked back into the kitchen. Peg was doing the dishes. "I'm going to find one of the men," he said, "to take charge here until I get you safely back in Banister."

"I'm not going," she said stubbornly.

He gripped her by the shoulder and turned her around. "Listen, young lady," he said harshly, "I've listened to enough of your opinions! Now you listen to mine! You can't stay out here on the F Bar M, unchaperoned, as Amy Chapman might say! I've got work to do and I can't get it done worrying about you. Now get ready to go back to Banister!"

"I won't!" she said hotly. "I'm staying here with you. I ..." Her mouth was closed

133

by a firm kiss. For a moment she was tense, then she relaxed and her arms crept slowly around his neck. The thought came suddenly to Vic that maybe this was the way he should have handled her a year ago, rather than to argue with her, then leave the country in a huff.

He left the house and rode out onto the range until he saw Jake Truro. He gave the man instructions and then returned to the house just as the sun slanted down over the western hills. Peg was ready. The two of them rode towards the crossing of Piney Creek. Vic wanted her safely in Banister before dusk.

There was no incident on the ride into Banister, in fact it was very pleasant despite the peril that was haunting them. It did one thing for Vic Standish. He was determined to get at the root of the trouble before there were any more killings, for he knew as surely as he was seated in his saddle, that he, and perhaps even Peg Earnshaw might be next in line to house a 700 grain Sharps slug.

He did not ride with Peg to Amy Chapman's boarding house. He had no frame of mind to face Amy when she was under the full sail of her imposing *respectability*. He left his horse at the livery stable and left by the rear entrance. He was almost to the corner of Mineral Street when a man called to him from a passageway between two buildings. It was dark now, the full darkness before the rising of the moon, but Vic recognized the voice. It was that of Ben Cullen. Vic turned quickly, dropping his hand to the butt of his Colt. Ben had picked his position well, for Vic could hardly see the man, nor could he see any weapon that Ben might have in his hands.

"What's wrong, Vic?" asked Ben.

"This is a helluva way to accost a man, Ben," said Vic coldly.

The marshal hesitated. "I wanted to talk with you."

Vic moved a little to one side to get a better look at the man. "Talk then," he said.

Ben came out into the open. There was no weapon in his hands. "Damn you, Vic," he said. "What's wrong with you?"

"I think you know well enough, Ben."

Ben looked up and down the deserted alleyway. "You mean that shotgun ambush of course?"

"Of course."

Ben came closer. "Listen, Vic, I knew that was riling you, and well it should rile you. I didn't know that sawed off scattergun was missing from my office until I saw it lying beside that house. I got rattled. I threw it into the barrel so I could think clearly."

"Why?" prodded Vic.

Ben smiled. "I guess you know by now I've been working on some deals with Jason Kile, but by Godfrey, Vic, it wasn't him, or any of his boys, or *me*, that tried to kill you that night."

Vic nodded. "I have been wondering how any of you could have beaten me over to Third Street."

Ben lowered his voice. "The scattergun was stolen from my gun rack in the office. I had a drunk in a cell. He said he saw a man come into the office and take the gun. Later that night Doc Parch tipped me off that a man had come into his office to get treated for a flesh wound. Claimed he had dropped his cocked pistol and had wounded himself. The man that took the shotgun and the man who was treated by Doc Parch was the same man, Vic."

Vic leaned closer to Ben. "Who was it?"

Ben placed a hand on Vic's shoulder. "I want no trouble. Let me take care of him. I just wanted you to know it wasn't me or any of the Kile bunch that did it."

"Who was it, Ben?"

Ben hesitated. "Promise me you'll let the law take its course?"

"Tell me, Ben!"

136

"Promise?"

Vic nodded.

"Dick Chapman," said Ben quietly.

Dick's hatred for Vic came back to Vic in a rush. Vic had shamed him the day of the funeral. It might have been better if Vic had killed him then and there, for Dick would never forgive him for that incident. Hurting a man's ego can make a vindictive enemy out of him, and Dick Chapman's ego was king sized. Peggy had told Vic that Dick could be dangerous, and not to underestimate him. That was exactly what Vic had done. "What are you going to do about it, Ben?" asked Vic.

Ben shrugged. "Arrest him. For two reasons, the first of which is that I want to have him hauled into court for what he did."

"And the second?"

Ben looked steadily at Vic. "I want to stop a killing in Banister, Vic."

"So long as we are being so honest with each other, and you've admitted working on deals, as you call them, with Jason Kile, can you tell me why Kile wants the Lazy E so badly?"

"You're not exactly the man I'd want to talk about that with."

"Forget the shiftiness, Ben. This is a

matter of murder! Good men have been slaughtered because someone wants that ranch. Why? Is Kile behind these killings?"

Ben hesitated. He looked up and down the alleyway. "Take it easy, Vic," he said. He didn't expect the gun muzzle that was rammed into his belly. He turned his head to look into Vic's cold eyes. "For God's sake, Vic! You loco?"

"Talk," said Vic.

Ben swallowed. "Kile really wants the F Bar M, and the two ranches beyond it, but he knows Jim Fancher would hold him up on the price of the F Bar M, and he happens to know too that Jim has options to buy both of those other ranches. You know Jim. He's a good man with a dollar. But Jim has been talking about selling. Kile played it smooth by pretending he was interested in the Lazy E and nothing else. He figured Jim would get scared that he couldn't sell the F Bar M when he had a buyer with ready cash. So Kile has been sitting back waiting for Jim to crack on his price."

"Is that all?" Vic holstered his Colt. "Don't lie to me, Ben."

The marshal shook his head. "Sure, it looks like Kile was behind the Earnshaw killings. But Forrie Cooke was practically challenged to a draw by Norm Earnshaw.

Cooke had definite orders not to get into gunfights. Kile used him as more of a threat than a killer. It was the same way in the fight between Chuck Budd and Nick Earnshaw. Budd could hardly have planned to kill Nick by driving him against that spike."

"I never could buy that business of that fight being rigged."

"Look, Vic! Kile is too shrewd to go around having people murdered to gain his ends. He had enough trouble in the Pioche country without tryng to get involved around here. Sure, I work with him, but only on the condition that he keeps peace around Banister. I owe *that* much to my job!"

Vic eyed the lawman. He was inclined to believe him.

"Besides," said Ben, "I've been approached by certain people concerning that sheriff's job; the one that Cranmer might lose. Kile is working for the deal along with certain others in the county. Do you think Kile would jeopardize a deal like that just on account of trying to get his hands on a second rate ranch like the Lazy E? It don't make sense!"

Vic felt for the makings. The politician in Ben was talking now, and it made good sense. Vic rolled a cigarette and lighted it. He handed the makings to Ben. "I don't want to kill Dick Chapman," said Vic quietly. "I don't want to do any killing at all. But you'd better put Dick behind bars, Ben. Tonight. Now!"

Ben nodded. "Fair enough, Vic. Now do me a favour! Don't go on a witch hunt here in Banister. I talked Jason Kile into leaving you alone. Fact of the matter is that Jason has a sort of grudging respect for you since you gave his two best boys a comeuppance in the Banister House Bar the other night."

"I was damned lucky," said Vic.

"I agree. I know you were close to the Earnshaws and I know how you feel about Peggy Earnshaw, but starting trouble with Kile and his corrida will get you nothing but double-barrelled trouble. Kile has agreed to forget about what happened. I expect you to do the same. Agreed?"

There was a ring of truth and sincerity in Ben's voice. Vic held out his hand and the marshal gripped it. They parted and Vic walked slowly up Mineral Street, intent on his thoughts, ignoring the women who called to him from the open windows of the bawdy houses. He didn't see one of the girls call over her naked shoulder to a man in the room behind her. He didn't see that man leave the house and run up the alleyway, parallel to the direction Vic was walking on the next street.

Things were still in a chaotic stage in his teeming mind. Forrie Cooke and Chuck Budd had been with him the night he had gone to get the bodies of the two murdered Earnshaws. That, in itself, didn't mean that they were not mixed up in the killings, but later that night, after Joe Dunlap had been so badly frightened by the shot that had come out of the darkness to shatter the lantern beside him, both Kile men had had the clear chance of shooting him down in cold blood, and neither of them had taken the opportunity.

Kile wanted no more trouble than necessary in that country. It *was* possible, from what Vic had heard, that both Norm and Nick Earnshaw had died in fair enough fights. Coincidence it certainly was, but if Ben Cullen was right, and Vic was almost sure the marshal was not lying about it, Kile was not behind the Earnshaw killings.

He reached the dark corner and stopped to roll a cigarette. He suddenly felt, rather than saw, a movement in the darkness of a doorway across the street. A cold feeling came over him, for the distant light from a street lamp suddenly reflected from metal. Metal shaped like a gun barrel. Then a tall man stepped out from the doorway, Colt cocked and ready in his hands. "Standish,"

141

he said. "They say you've got one of the fastest draws in Nevada. Let's see it, big man."

It was Dick Chapman and the cold light of hate was in his eyes.

Boots grated on the street. A man rounded the corner, and ran towards Chapman. "Dick?" he said. "Dick Chapman! Put up that gun. You're under arrest!" It was Ben Cullen.

Chapman did not look away from Vic. "On what charges, Cullen?"

"Attempted murder. You stole a shotgun from my office and attempted to kill Vic Standish."

Chapman laughed. "You're loco, Cullen."

"Standish said he wounded whoever shot at him. Doc Parch says he treated you for a flesh wound that same night. Put up that gun, Chapman. Surrender quietly."

"Go to hell!" snarled Chapman. He turned to fire at Ben. Ben clawed for his Colt. Chapman fired. The slug whipped Cullen's hat from his head. The man staggered back, trying to draw his Colt. Chapman crouched and aimed again. Vic's hand swept down. He drew, cocked and fired. The Colt bucked back into his hand. Dick Chapman screamed hoarsely as the slug shattered his right wrist.

142

He went down on his knees screaming like a woman.

Ben drew his Colt at last. "All right, Chapman," he said. "This adds another charge of attempted murder." The marshal looked at Vic. "Thanks, Vic. He had me cold."

Vic holstered his Colt. "You ought to lubricate that holster, Ben, and practise a few draws."

"Yeh," said Ben shamefacedly. "You can go, Vic. I'll take him in. I'll need you as witness for this attempt."

"Pleased," said Vic. He watched Ben lead away the wounded man. A curious crowd had begun to gather. Vic walked back into the alleyway. It had been too close for comfort. He rounded the corner and walked into the Nevada Joy and ordered rye. The place was almost empty, but a drunk was babbling in a rear booth. Somehow the voice sounded familiar. Vic turned to look at him. It was Ace Miles, drunk as sin. Vic took the bottle and his glass to the booth and looked down at Ace. The cowpoke looked blearily up at him. "You buying?" he said.

Vic nodded. He sat down and filled the glasses. "You sure made tracks out of there the night of the fire, Ace," he said quietly.

Ace wiped his mouth on his sleeve. "Didn' wanna get mixed up," he said thickly.

"Maybe you know more than what you let on."

Ace hiccupped. His eyes widened. "Meaning what?"

"Who set that fire in the barn, Ace?"

"I don't know."

Vic looked back over his shoulder. He gripped Ace by the arm and steered the little man out the back door of the saloon. He shoved Ace back against the rear wall of the saloon. "It was Carl Rivera, wasn't it?" he demanded.

Ace passed a dirty hand across his eyes. "I said I wasn't going to talk!" he said.

Vic banged the little man's head back against the wall. "Tell me!" he said harshly.

"All right! All right! I ain't gettin' nothin' out of the deal anyhow."

Vic stepped back and as he did so he heard the grating of feet in the darkness of the alleyway to his right. He jumped back and reached for his Colt.

"It was..." Ace's voice was cut short in a blast of flame and smoke. He pitched forward on his face just as Vic dropped belly flat and thrust his pistol forward. Boots grated again down the smokey alley. Vic fired just once, knowing it was wild. The sound

144

of running feet died away. A man shouted from the other end of the alleyway. Vic darted through a passageway between the saloon and the livery stable where he had left his horse. Just as he slipped inside the livery stable he heard the saloon door bang open and a man yell out. "Marshal! Marshal Cullen! Someone get the marshal! Vic Standish just shot Ace Miles to death in the alleyway!"

There was no time to lose. Vic led his horse from its stall and mounted it. There were no witnesses to the death of the little cowpoke. Vic would have to be jailed until he could prove he was innocent and that might take time. He might not even clear himself. He had other things to do. A dangerous killer was haunting that country. One man alone was tying together the threads, the clues that might just lead him to the killer before the pattern was completed. That man was Vic Standish.

He spurred the horse through the doorway and sank the steel into it again. Men scattered as he raced down the centre of the street.

"It's Standish!" yelled Chuck Budd.

"After him!" yelled Forrie Cooke.

The last thing Vic saw was the cold, unsmiling face of Jason Kile, as the man stood outside the Banister House Bar, watching Vic Standish ride for his life and freedom, then Vic was hammering over the bridge headed for Piney Creek. It would only be a matter of minutes before a posse would form. Kile had not forgotten Vic Standish. Kile men would form part of that posse. The answer was obvious.

He turned in the saddle as he reached the far side of the river. Men were mounting horses in the street. Men were yelling and calling out to each other. Men who would hunt down Vic Standish as though he was really a killer. There was no recognized law in the county. A rope or a bullet would take care of Vic Standish. There were plenty of men in Banister who'd like to see him out of the way.

The horse stretched out, racing along the dark road. Vic cursed to himself. Ace Miles had been within a split second of talking when his voice had been stilled forever by a killer's bullet.

Vic reached down for his Winchester. His questing hand struck an empty scabbard. He had either lost the gun in the stable or someone had taken it. He couldn't fight without a rifle. There was one place he could get one, if he could outrace his pursuers. That was the F Bar M.

Vic turned the horse savagely and cut across a meadowland to a grove of woods. He raced through the grove, leaped a wall, splashed through a stream, then cut straight across country for the ranch. The shortcut would save him five or ten minutes. Just time enough to arm himself and grab some grub in case he had to hole up in the hills.

Chapter Ten

The moon was just rising above the eastern range when Vic Standish reined in his lathered horse behind the F Bar M barn. He ripped the saddle from the tired horse and ran to the corral. He roped and saddled a blocky claybank. As he worked he kept his ears attuned to the night sounds. There was just time to get what he wanted and pull foot out of there. He snatched up a sack from the barn and ran into the house. There wasn't a sign of life about the place. He stuffed the sack with food, dropped it on the rear porch, then darted into the living-room. There were several weapons racked in there, shotguns and Winchesters, and an old Spencer repeater. Vic ripped a Winchester .44/40 from the rack. He'd need cartridges. He ran to a closet where Jim kept all kinds of odds and ends, as well as his ammunition supplies. Vic grabbed two fresh boxes of .44/40 and ran towards Jim's bedroom. He'd need a blanket or two if he had to hole up.

He tore open a closet door and grabbed two blankets. There was a little snow on the mountain tops, forecasting a cold fall and hard winter. He'd need a jacket. He reached into the closet, felt the thick material of a woollen coat and tore it from the hook. He raced back through the house, snatched some matches and carton of makings from the pantry shelf and grabbed up his food sack as he ran across the sagging porch.

The moon was shining down on the ranch as he fastened his things to the saddle, then swung up onto the claybank. It was then that his ears caught the steady tattoo of hoofs on the road beyond Piney Creek. He sank the steel into the claybank and thundered across the yard behind the barn clearing the fence with nothing to spare. He rode into a motte of willows and cottonwoods, then splashed across a shallow brook. The claybank was a goer. He ran as though his life, as well as that of his rider, depended on his strength and speed.

Vic reached the boundary line between the
148

F Bar M and the Lazy E. As he rode up a ridge he looked back across the lower country towards the ranch buildings he had just left. Lights flickered about the place. The wind carried the sound of voices to him.

He spurred the claybank and turned it towards the rugged hills that separated the range from the Valley of the Skull. There were plenty of hiding places in those hills where a man would be safe enough for a time at least. Time to think and plan his way.

It was dawn when Vic awoke. He threw aside the blankets and peered out of the shallow cave in which he had spent the quiet night. A mist hung in the canyon below him. He ate cold beef and hard bread, sipped some water, rolled a cigarette, then squatted at the mouth of the cave with his rifle across his thighs. He could make a break from the hill country, but the telegraph would race ahead of him with his description. Meanwhile the posse might be beating up the local area, searching high and low for him.

Try as he would, his fears for his own safety were constantly being relegated to second place in his thoughts. The bloody mystery that was haunting the Skull Valley country constantly usurped precedence in his mind. Somehow he knew that if he solved that mystery he'd be able to clear himself of the murder of Ace Miles.

He piled his gear in the back of the cave, then walked down to the claybank. He had left the horse picketed in a hidden box canyon. There was a shallow waterhole there and some grazing, enough for a few days at least. Vic threaded his way east from the canyon and worked his way silently towards the Valley of the Skull.

The sun was full up when he lay bellyflat on the rim of the west side of the canyon. Directly across from him was the looming skull formation, lighted by the sun. Vic kept a cigarette cupped in his hand as he studied the quiet valley. The sun flashed from the ripples of the creek. It shone on the blackened beds of ashes where the fires had destroyed the Lazy E buildings. It was quiet and peaceful, too quiet and peaceful to suit Vic Standish. He uncased his battered fieldglasses and focused them on the narrow mouth of the creek pass. There was no sign of life there. He scanned the opposite escarpment until he reached the skull formation. Foot by foot he studied that grotesque formation. It seemed to him there was greater depth within the eyes of the skull than he had ever realized. There surely was a way of getting inside that eerie formation.

Vic lowered the glasses and took a drag from his cigarette. In his mind that formation was part of the disjointed puzzle he was trying to solve.

He snubbed out the cigarette and worked his way down the steep crumbling side of the valley until he could take cover within the trees that edged the valley wall. He worked his way north towards the bridge, then lay down in the brush to study the valley again. If anyone was watching from the heights they could hardly miss seeing a man cross that sunlit valley.

He'd have to wait until dusk at least. Meanwhile the hunt would still be on, with Vic Standish the prize. He had never felt so alone in all his life.

The sun was slanting down into the Valley of the Skull when the wind shifted and carried the sound of voices to Vic. He looked across the valley and saw two people leading horses down the trail that slanted across the crumbling face of the valley's eastern wall. He felt for his glasses and focused them on the two people. His heart leaped when he saw the lovely face of Peggy Earnshaw. Joe Dunlap was with her. Vic would no longer be alone if he chose to speak to them.

They had crossed the bridge when he whistled softly from the woods. Peggy's head turned. She saw Vic's head and shoulders protruding from the brush. A moment later she was tearing up the slope to the man she loved.

Joe Dunlap was all grins as he watched them. "My God," he said to Vic. "Banister was like a beehive last night! Jason Kile and his boys had everyone organized to get you, Vic. Whereinell did you get to?"

Vic shrugged. "I know the hills, Joe," he said.

Peggy passed a smooth hand across his bristly cheek. "My heart went with you last night, Vic. I wanted to come after you alone, but Joe came to me and said he'd help me."

Joe nodded. "We know you didn't kill Ace, but the way Kile and his boys were talking last night, they meant to string you up first, then ask questions later. We'll help you get out of this country as quickly as you can, then I'll see what I can do about getting this thing straightened out. You got any idea who killed Ace?"

"I never saw the killer," said Vic. He looked up and down the valley. "We'd better get out of here. I'll show you my hideout."

He led them up the western wall of the valley just as the sun dropped behind the western ranges, dipping the valley into shadowy darkness. It was still light on the

152

heights above the valley as he led them to the box canyon to picket their horses and then to his cave. He made a fire of dried wood and roasted meat for them. The three of them sat in the cave chewing the stringy beef while the darkness decended fully on the hills.

Joe swallowed. He felt for the makings.

"Don't light up, Joe," said Vic. "A man could see the burning end of a cigarette for half a mile in here."

"Yeh, yeh," said Joe. He grinned. "Forgot we was on the run."

Vic handed Peggy a blanket to wrap around her shoulders. Despite the ever present danger he felt a glow of comfort having them with them, even Joe Dunlap, drunk that he was, but the man seemed sober enough this night.

Joe leaned back against the side of the cave. "We can work out a way to smuggle you out of this country. Head for Mexico maybe."

"No," said Vic. He sipped his coffee. "I'm sticking until I find out who is behind these killings."

"That's loco!" said Joe.

Peggy nodded. "Joe is right," she agreed.

"If I run and keep on running," said Vic, "I'll never be able to clear myself. I think that if I can find the man who has been behind these killings, I can clear myself. If I run now, I'll never get another chance."

"The whole country is thick with possemen," said Joe.

Vic grinned a little. "They haven't found me yet."

Joe nodded. "No, Vic, but it's only a matter of time. There's something else. By staying around here, you're endangering Peg. I can't stand for that."

Vic looked up quickly. "Is that a fact? Well, Mister Dunlap, I don't give a damn what you can't stand for."

Joe flushed. "I was only trying to protect Peg, Vic."

"Let me worry about that." Vic said. "We'd better check the horses."

Joe picked up his rifle and left the cave.

"He means well," said Peggy quietly.

Vic drew her close and kissed her. "You're my concern now, Peg. I've got to do what I think is best. Trust me."

"I always have," she said simply.

Vic followed Joe down the dark slope. There was a faint trace of the rising moon in the eastern sky. Joe turned as they reached the box canyon. "I'll ask you once more to leave the country, Vic," he pleaded.

"I'm staying, Joe."

Joe shook his head. "I'm the last of Peg's

kin, Vic. Maybe they mean to kill me too, but I've got to think of Peg. You remember the night that killer smashed the lantern next to me? That was a sure enough warning. I'll stick through, Vic. It's my duty."

Vic smiled. He placed a hand on Joe's shoulder. "I know you mean well, Joe, but I can't leave now."

Vic walked up the canyon. He shifted the horses so that they could reach the water hole. The moonlight was just illuminating the upper walls of the box canyon when he was done. He turned to speak to Joe. The man was gone. Vic walked towards the mouth of the canyon. His eyes probed into the thick darkness in the lower part of the canyon. Maybe the man had lost his nerve and run out despite his brave words.

Something was wrong. The feeling came slowly over Vic. He looked back up the canyon. The moonlight glistened on the waterhole. The horses were quietly grazing. Vic started forward again, then stopped. He peered towards a jumble of rocks and brush on the right hand side of the canyon entrance. There was a place there where the shadows looked thicker. He stared at it. He laughed softly. "Getting jittery," he said.

He was almost within the canyon mouth when the rifle crashed deafeningly within fifty yards of him. The slug passed within a hairsbreadth of his right ear. He hit the ground, rolled over and over, levering a round into his Winchester as he did so, then squirmed behind a rock ledge. The rifle crashed again and the slug screamed eerily as it glanced from the rock ledge a foot from Vic's head. Vic fired once, ducked down, reloaded, then bellied along the harsh ground to the end of the ledge where he lay still, nothing more than a lean shadow that seemed part of the ledge itself.

Minutes ticked past. Vic wet his dry lips as he studied the far side of the canyon. Time passed. Then he heard a soft grating noise. A shadow flitted from one bush to another. Vic moved his rifle a little. The shadow reached the canyon floor. It started across. The moonlight showed on the taught, frightened face of Joe Dunlap. He peered at the ledge.

"Joe!" said Vic. "Throw down that gun!"

Joe whirled and fired from the hip. The slug slashed rock shards and bits of lead against Vic's hat. Vic fired once. Joe grunted in savage pain. He bent over and whirled about, falling heavily. He lay still.

Vic walked towards him, levering a fresh

round into his smoking rifle. "Joe," he said. He came closer.

Joe Dunlap made his play. He thrust his Colt forwards and fired. The slug whipped through the slack in Vic's shirt. Vic's slug caught the man in the chest. Joe screamed hoarsely. Blood spated from his squared mouth and he fell forward to lie still once more.

Vic rolled him over. The man's eyes were wide and already beginning to glaze. "Joe," said Vic. "Who is behind this thing?"

Joe trembled. His fingers dug into the hard ground.

"Joe?" said Vic. "You're dying. Tell me, for God's sake! Clear yourself. Do this thing for Peg if not for me. Who is it, Joe?"

"He said...he'd kill...me...if I didn't help...him."

"Who, Joe?"

"He'd do it too."

"Tell me, Joe!"

Joe Dunlap lay still. Then his breathing became harsh and irregular. "I've always hated the Earnshaws," he said clearly. "I was always...the weak sister. I've always hated you, Standish. Find out for yourself...you sonofabitch. My sand has run out. But... he'll get you..." The man coughed thickly.

"He's lookin' for...you...now..." Then Joe Dunlap was gone forever.

Vic stood up and wiped the cold sweat from his forehead. He looked up to see Peggy Earnshaw walking silently towards him. "Stay back," he said quickly.

"I heard the shooting," she said. "I heard Joe's last words. What does it mean, Vic?"

"I don't know. I'm tired of fighting a phantom. Joe said *he*, whoever *he* is, is looking for me now. Well, I'm going to look for him!"

He heaved Joe's body into a cleft and covered it with loose rock, then walked with Peg to the cave through the darkness of the bigger canyon, as it was not yet lighted by the moon. Swiftly they gathered their gear together. Vic handed the girl the thick woollen jacket he had taken from the ranch house. She shrugged into it, then followed him through the darkness to the box canyon.

Vic got two of the horses and led them to the girl. She was fingering the jacket he had given her. "What kind of a coat is this, Vic?" she asked curiously.

He eyed it casually. "Looks like a Civil War blouse," he said. "In fact, I'm sure it is."

"A *green* Civil War blouse, Vic?"

Vic eyed it. In the moonlight it was difficult at first to tell the exact shade of the jacket, but there wasn't any doubt but that it was green in hue, and of Civil War cut.

"I've never seen one this colour before," she said. She laughed. "Not that it matters. Maybe it was dyed."

"Yeh," said Vic quietly. A strange feeling came over him as he looked at that jacket, relic of the War Between the States. The Blue and the Grey. Not green. Why would a Civil War jacket be dyed green?

"Where to?" she asked.

Vic looked east. "Back there," he said.

"It's too dangerous, Vic."

"I think the answer is back there. I am almost sure of it."

They rode towards the mouth of the box canyon, past the place where Joe Dunlap was stiffening in death, with his secret still locked within his dead mind.

Vic could not look at Peggy. She was the last of the Earnshaws now, the last survivor of the Fightng Earnshaws, men who had fought and died with their boots on.

The Valley of the Skull was well lighted by the moon. It was as peaceful a nocturnal scene as one could wish, with the creek a silvery ribbon, the dark shadows of the trees etched on the ground, a whispering wind drifting down the valley, moaning softly in the creek pass.

They tethered their horses in the bosque not far from the bridge. It was so quiet and peaceful Vic could almost believe there had been no bloodshed there in days past, but he knew in his mind that the valley was haunted by someone who could deal out death with the ease of a professional. He looked again at the green jacket the girl wore. Something was trying to get through to his mind. Something he had heard long ago, in his pre-school days; something his father had told him. Vic squatted beside the girl and looked across the valley towards the bright rounded shape of the rock skull. The thought in his mind, and the skull formation were inextricably tangled in his thoughts and yet he knew nothing he could pin down to reality.

"Look!" said Peggy.

Vic looked across the valley just in time to see a man moving about amongst the rocks to the south of the skull formation, a man carrying a long barrelled rifle. The coldness of reality drove his wandering thoughts from his mind. The man vanished as suddenly as he had appeared. Vic's impulse was to cross the creek but he remembered all too well the night he had been creased by bark chips from the tree below the skull.

Vic turned to speak to Peggy and as he did so his nerves were badly shaken, for the eyes of the skull seemed to light up with a hellish glow from within, then the light died away to be replaced with a faint and flickering light from *within* the skull.

Vic stood up. "I'm going over there," he said.

"Not alone, Vic."

"Yes, Peg."

She firmly shook her head. "Where you go, I go. This is my fight as well as yours. I'm the last of the Earnshaws, Vic. I can go down fighting as well as the rest of them."

There was no argument. Vic led the way through the trees, north towards the ford, still hidden in shadows from the overhanging cottonwoods and willows. He led the girl through the rustling brush until they found the escarpment trail. They ascended, just in time, for at any minute the moon would move further west and would light the trail.

Vic crouched down in the tangled masses of rock and brush within a hundred yards of the skull. It was quiet except for the rustling of the brush and the whispering of the wind. There was no way they could see if the skull was still occupied.

161

"Stay here," whispered Vic. He padded forward and worked his way to the south side of the skull. Back and forth he worked with the uncanny feeling that the skull was eying him coldly over its rock shoulder when he wasn't looking. Several times he caught himself snapping a look towards the formation, half expecting to see it look quickly away.

He was about to give up when his left boot sank into a soft pocket of earth. He looked down. There were other boot prints plainly to be seen, fresh, and pointed towards what looked like a long crack in a huge, tiptilted boulder. He walked to it. Brush mantled the side of it. He pushed his way through and a cold draught played about his face. Vic worked his way forward in a deep cleft, then saw the dark mouth of a tunnel just ahead of him. There was no sight nor sound of life from within.

"Vic?"

He turned quickly to see the tense, white face of Peggy. "Go back!" he said sharply.

"No."

There wasn't any use in arguing with her and it wasn't quite the place to do so in any case. Vic leaned his rifle against the side of the passageway and drew his Colt. He eased forward towards the tunnel. He felt his way

162

inside of it and his right foot bumped something metallic. He knelt and felt about. His hand touched a large can. He lifted it and held it so that the moonlight would strike it. The letters stood out clearly: Golden Pheasant Gun Powder. The can was empty.

Vic moved forward, feeling his way through the winding tunnel that wound like a labyrinth deeper and deeper into the skull. Now and then he would stop and listen, with Peg pressed close behind him, but he heard nothing except the wind.

The light struck him so unexpectedly when he rounded a turn in the tunnel that he almost cried out in surprise. He stopped, looking in a rough cavern ahead of him. A crude table stood there, with a candle guttering in the neck of a bottle. He looked at Peg and shook his head, warning her to stay put. Vic padded forward. The table was littered with reloading tools, empty brass cartridge cases, primers and other necessaries for reloading. To one side was another can of Golden Pheasant Powder. It was half empty. The cartridge cases were un-mistakable. They were for the huge 700 grain slug of the Sharps Big Fifty.

He looked towards the dark mouth of yet another tunnel, and as he did so he heard the dull thudding noise, as though someone was

163

digging. Vic led the way into the tunnel. It branched, then branched again, as he felt his way along, and he kept moving through the draughty darkness by sheer instinct, trying to keep the sound of the digging in his hearing as a guide. He was about to give up when he saw the indistinct flickering of light ahead of him. As he walked softly towards it he saw can after can of powder piled against the side of the tunnel, but this time it wasn't powder for reloading rifle cartridges, but rather blasting powder, Kepauno Chemical Company Giant Blasting powder. It was the best. One match dropped amidst those cans might cause an explosion that would blow the skull formation clear down into the creek far below.

The digging sound was louder now. Vic held back Peg with an open hand and shook his head. He padded forward until he could see the grotesque shadow of the working man cast upon the rough wall of the large cavern in which he was digging. A long-barrelled rifle leaned against the wall. There was no doubt but what it was a Sharps, probably the most accurate singleshot rifle of its time.

Vic eyed that mysterious shadow; quite likely the shadow of the deadly marksman who had killed Buck Earnshaw, and probably Mark Earnshaw as well; Little Mac, Jim

Fancher's beloved partner; Carl Rivera, and quite possibly Ace Miles. Vic moved a little closer, trying to locate the man rather than the shadow. Peg moved close up behind him. He could not stop her, nor speak to her now. If that unseen man was the killer Vic suspected him to be, there would be little time to shoot fast and accurately. If he once got his hands on that deadly rifle...

Vic moved forward. His foot struck an empty can. The digging sound stopped. For a fraction of a second there was frozen silence within the huge skull formation. Then the man appeared, snatching up the Sharps with one hand, striking out the light with the other, and in that fraction of a second Vic saw the indistinct face, before shrouding darkness and deadly peril descended into the black tunnel.

Boots grated on rock. Metal rang as it struck rock. Then the sound of the boots faded away.

Vic knew it was no use in trying to feel his way after the fugitive. Even if he found him he'd likely find a Sharps slug as well.

Peg came close to him, shivering against him. There was a bitter coldness within Vic and not all of it came from the damp cold of the naked rock which surrounded them. He thought he should know that vague face he had seen. His hand drew Peg closer and he felt the thick wool of the blouse. Then he remembered what his father had told him long ago, of a day in July of 1863, when Confederate troops of Longstreet's First Corps had struck the Union left at Gettysburg, opposed by a handful of men. Vic's father had been a cavalry courier whose horse had been killed, and Vic's father had been wounded. He was lying on the field when the Confederate attack had begun. Time after time Alabama troops, the fighting cocks of the First Corps had charged against the handful of Union troops, only to be hurled back again and again by the deadly rifle fire. Fire from long-barrelled Sharps singleshot rifles. It was one hundred of Berdan's First United States Sharpshooters, supported by two hundred men of the Third Maine, who had held that exposed Union flank. The finest riflemen in the Army of the Potomac. In the time they had held the Union right, there had been opportunity for fresh troops to be rushed to defend Little Round Top, in the narrowest escape from defeat in three days of many narrow escapes.

"Berdan's First United States Sharpshooters," said Vic quietly. He passed a hand over the thick wool of the green blouse.

Berdan's two regiments of marksmen had worn green uniforms to blend with woods, brush and grass. The deadliest marksmen in the Army of the Potomac.

"What is wrong, Vic?" asked Peg.

Vic raised his head. "I think I know who I am looking for now, Peg," he said. "Stay here." He pulled off his boots and took off his hat. With his Colt in his hand he began to feel his way through the darkness in that hellish natural labyrinth haunted by a professional killer.

Chapter Eleven

Vic wet his lips. He pressed back into a niche in the tunnel wall. "Jim?" he called out. "Jim Fancher!"

The darkness echoed his cry. *"Jim? Jim? Jim? Jim Fancher! Jim Fancher! Jim Fancher! Fancher! Fancher! Fancher!"* Then it died away.

There was a long silence.

"Jim?" called Vic again.

Something moved in the thick darkness down the tunnel, between Vic and the only known way to escape from within the skull.

"I'll have to kill you now, Vic," said Jim Fancher.

Vic had never known Jim Fancher to carry a pistol. He had always looked down upon the short gun. All he had ever carried was a Winchester in a saddle scabbard. "You've only got one round in that Sharps, Jim," said Vic.

The rancher laughed. "You think I need more than one round?"

The man could shoot the long gun better than any man Vic had ever known. He had supreme confidence in his warped mind. "Give yourself up, Jim," said Vic. "You'll get a fair trial."

Fancher laughed. "After all those killings? One is enough to hang me."

"How many of them did you do?" said Vic. He worked a little closer as soon as he heard Jim speak.

"Little Mac knew too much. He was in my way. Mark Earnshaw was too stubborn to sell out when I tried to get the Lazy E. I killed him with a Winchester and Buck with my Sharps so as to make it look like more than one man was doing the killings."

"And Carl Rivera?" asked Vic, stalling for time.

"I was aiming near you, Vic, to scare you. Carl got in the way."

"Like you tried to scare Joe Dunlap?"

"Joe knew about me, and so did Carl and Ace. I had to shut Ace up."

"You had plenty of chances to kill me, Jim, and Peg as well."

There was a long pause.

"I didn't want to kill you, Vic. I figured you'd work with me some day. You were like a son to me. I ain't never killed a woman, and I didn't want to start."

"And now?"

There was another pause. "You figure that one out, Vic."

Cold sweat trickled down Vic's sides. Jim was mad. He was a homicidal maniac and a dead shot as well. If Vic didn't kill Jim, he'd kill Vic and Peg as well. There was no way out of that trap unless Vic killed the man. He closed his eyes and shook his head, remembering the many kindnesses Jim had done for him. He had almost been like a father to Vic. "But why, Jim?" he asked.

"Stay where you are! I got ears like an Apache. This rifle is aimed by sound in here, Vic."

Vic stopped moving. He believed the older man.

Jim laughed. "Why?" he jeered. "You're inside one of the finest deposits of ruby copper I've ever seen in the whole of

169

Nevada! This deposit will make me a rich man, Vic." He paused. "It could have been a partnership with me and you."

Vic tried to pierce the darkness with his eyes. He was almost sure he could see something ahead of him, and then he realized that somehow the faint rays of the moon were penetrating from reflection inside part of the skull at least.

"Amy wouldn't live on the ranch," continued Jim, almost as though talking to himself. "She wanted money. Lots of money. More than I had. I found this place almost six months ago. To make sure I began to work it, tracing the vein. It's priceless, Vic!"

Vic raised his Colt. He wasn't sure if the shadow he saw was Jim or not, but he had six cartridges to expend as opposed to the one Jim had.

"I had to have the ranch, Vic. I got rid of two of the Earnshaws and two more of them conveniently got themselves killed. Damned fools! I done *my* fighting in the war. I had a bellyfull of it, but this was worth fighting for in the only way I knew how. I figured Peg would get married and I'd force Joe Dunlap into selling his share to me, and I'd make damned sure I'd get this part of the Lazy E.

Well, it'll be mine now. Amy will marry me now."

Vic made his play. He jumped forward and fired, then dropped flat. The Sharps roared like a brass Napoleon cannon in the narrow confines of the tunnel and the slug plucked at Vic's hair. Jim yelled hoarsely. The tunnel was thick with smoke. Vic fired four more rounds directly up the tunnel. The slugs screamed thinly from the rock walls, slamming around in ricochet inside the area where Jim Fancher was trying to reload. There was a hoarse screaming sound, and then silence.

Vic coughed as the powdersmoke swirled about him. He walked forward and his feet struck a body. He lighted a match and looked down into the bloody, shapeless face of Jim Fancher, destroyed by a softnosed, mutilated slug.

Vic hauled the body and the rifle outside, along the escarpment in the silvery moonlight. He looked at the horrible grinning face of the skull that had dominated the valley for so many years. Peggy came out, palefaced and badly shaken. She took off the green sharpshooter's blouse and covered Jim's shattered face with it. He had worn that in honour at least.

Vic walked back into that skull of hell. He

found a fuse and wire. He placed it in one of the big cans of blasting powder and lighted it, then ran from the skull. He held Peggy close to him. Then suddenly, with a subdued roaring noise that grew into an outburst of shattering sound the entire skull formation lifted from the solid rock and fell forward, sliding and grating down the face of the escarpment. Smoke and rock dust swirled through the valley that was no longer the Valley of the Skull. The copper vein could be worked better now. The Lazy E was the sole possession of Peggy Earnshaw, last of the Fighting Earnshaws.

They walked back to the trail; leaving Jim Fancher stiffening in death beneath the drifting dust of the rock formation for which he had killed and killed again, and then had paid the final price himself.

Neither of them looked back. To Peg Earnshaw and Vic Standish there was only *one* way to look. Forward, into the life they would live together.